"Dammit, Alex." Frustration roughened Zane's voice to a growl. "Everything's private with you, everything's too personal to share."

She drew back, stung.

"Some days I catch myself obsessing, what is she keeping from me? Then I think, *everything.* You say this part of a relationship is for getting to know one another, but whenever I try, you shut me out. You change the subject, you refuse to answer questions, you get hostile. And over the past couple of days, you kiss me or give me 'that look' and the question gets forgotten. I think I prefer the direct hostility. It feels more honest."

Tears blurred her vision. A dozen scathing replies came to mind, but she choked them all down. Because she'd been a fraud from day one. She didn't have the right to fight with him over it.

"I'm obviously not ready for this," she said. "Maybe I never will be. Maybe I'm damaged goods. You're a great guy, and you should hold out for someone with more to offer."

"Alex, wait—" He scrambled off the bed.

She paused in the doorway and gave him a sad smile. "On the bright side, you won't have to worry about my distracting you with kisses anymore."

Dear Reader,

I have enjoyed writing my Hill Country Heroes books almost as much as I enjoyed visiting the Texas Hill Country region! For my last book in the miniseries, I wanted to come up with a special hero, someone quintessentially Texan. Meet Zane Winchester, Texas Ranger, a brave lawman devoted to his community and his daughter. Unfortunately for Zane, sometimes raising a teenager can be just as tricky as tracking down bad guys.

Single mom Heather Hargrove is facing her own parenting challenges—namely how to keep her four-year-old out of the clutches of her wealthy and corrupt former in-laws. When desperation forces Heather into hiding under a false identity, she winds up living right next door to Zane. Just how is she supposed to keep her secrets from a man trained to solve cases and see through lies? Just as troubling, how is she supposed to keep herself from falling for the handsome neighbor who manages to make her laugh in the midst of her problems and values her advice as a parent?

Writing this book, I grew to care not only about Heather and Zane but their community of friends and family. Follow me on Twitter and Facebook to get the latest announcements on whether any of the characters might be popping up in future stories!

Happy reading,

Tanya

Rescued by a Ranger

TANYA MICHAELS

HARLEQUIN®
entertain, enrich, inspire™

PLEASE RECYCLE · THIS PRODUCT IS RECYCLABLE

Recycling programs
for this product may
not exist in your area.

ISBN-13: 978-0-373-75423-6

RESCUED BY A RANGER

www.Harlequin.com

Printed in U.S.A.

ABOUT THE AUTHOR

Three-time RITA® Award nominee Tanya Michaels writes about what she knows—community, family and lasting love! Her books, praised for their poignancy and humor, have received honors such as a Booksellers' Best Bet Award, a Maggie Award of Excellence and multiple readers' choice awards. She was also a 2010 *RT Book Reviews* nominee for Career Achievement in Category Romance. Tanya is an active member of Romance Writers of America and a frequent public speaker, presenting workshops to educate and encourage aspiring writers. She lives outside Atlanta with her very supportive husband, two highly imaginative children and a household of quirky pets, including a cat who thinks she's a dog and a bichon frise who thinks she's the center of the universe.

Books by Tanya Michaels
HARLEQUIN AMERICAN ROMANCE

HARLEQUIN TEMPTATION

*4 Seasons in Mistletoe
**Hill Country Heroes

It's important for writers to recharge creatively and stay inspired.

This book was powered by the music of NEEDTOBREATHE and Rob Thomas.

Chapter One

Oh, God, what have I done? Panic crowded Heather Hargrove's chest. Faced with the scariest threat of her life, she'd bolted—potentially making her circumstances even worse. In an attempt to calm herself, Heather watched her four-year-old daughter contentedly snore beneath a blanket on the leather sofa. *Josie's safe.* For the moment, anyway.

I won't let anyone take her from me.

Although they'd fled Houston earlier that day, the reality of Heather's situation was just as grim here in Dallas. She did not have the long-term resources to fight Eileen and Phillip Hargrove. Her wealthy former in-laws were one of the most powerful couples in the state of Texas. They'd be nearly impossible to beat in a custody battle even if they let themselves be constrained by anything as plebeian as "conscience" or "law." When Heather had first become engaged to their son, the Hargroves had attempted to end the relationship by bribing one of her former foster mothers to lie about her. With pockets as deep as theirs, who knew what kind of damaging testimony they could buy? If Heather had faced them in court, she would have lost Josie, her entire world. But her failure to appear this afternoon meant the judge could rule automatic forfeiture of custody.

"Here." Bryce Callahan walked back into the condo living room carrying two mugs. One was chipped at the top and featured a cartoon alien. The other was a shiny cobalt blue, printed with the logo of his software company. "Sorry I can't offer you anything to add to your coffee. I got used to drinking mine black because I never remember to buy sugar."

When she took the drink without comment, he added, "I did see a jug of milk behind the take-out boxes in the fridge, but I think it's been there since Christmas."

She tried unsuccessfully to smile. "You should probably throw it out, then."

"With St. Patrick's Day only three weeks away? Pshaw. It'll fit right in with all the other green beverages."

Heather cradled the warm mug between her hands. The last thing her jangled nerves needed was caffeine, but she was grateful for the heat. After the rainy five-hour drive, she felt frozen from the unrelenting damp and pervasive fear. "I'm sorry I came here, Bryce. I didn't really think this through." She'd been operating on desperation and adrenaline.

"Hey, what are old friends for? You don't have to apologize, Red." His crooked smile and the unimaginative nickname took her back to when she'd been eighteen. "I told you at that fundraiser to call me if you ever needed anything, remember?" Their chance encounter at a charity gala last April had been the one bright spot of a mortifying evening.

He'd handed her his business card, eyes filled with worry, and said he hoped to hear from her soon. Prior to that night, the two college friends hadn't seen each other since Bryce had flunked out of the University of Texas. The computer genius had prioritized all-nighters leveling up in video games above attending 8:00 a.m. sociology lectures.

Tonight, in plaid pajama pants and a black T-shirt boasting Total Domination, his sandy brown hair in need of a trim, Bryce looked more like the bighearted slacker he used to be than the successful game designer he was now. At the benefit, she hadn't even recognized him in his tux. Of course, she'd been preoccupied, trying to deal with her uncharacteristically hostile husband at the last social function they'd attended as a married couple. Unlike his father, Christopher Hargrove's favorite form of manipulation had always been charm, not bullying. But, by last spring, Christopher had become fed up with her questions about his family's shadier dealings and her insistence that they couldn't raise their daughter with the Hargroves' flagrant disregard for rules.

Christopher had believed consequences were for other people, but being rich, good-looking and well-connected hadn't saved him when he wrapped his sports car around a tree the month after Heather left him. The Hargroves blamed her, said his self-destructive actions had been fueled by his pain over losing his wife and daughter. Eileen Hargrove's ice blue eyes had bored holes into Heather at the funeral. *"You killed him, you ungrateful nobody. You killed my son! And you will pay."*

Heather shivered, and coffee sloshed over the rim of her mug.

"Easy," Bryce cautioned, taking the hot cup away from her. He turned to set it on the coffee table, but the surface was buried under gaming magazines, napkins from local fast-food restaurants and illegible notes scrawled in half a dozen spiral notebooks. With a shrug, he shoved a stack of papers to the floor, then blinked at the corner he'd uncovered. "Huh. I forgot this had a glass top."

"What am I going to do?" Heather asked. It was a rhetorical question. Her mess wasn't his problem.

"I'll tell you what you're *not* going to do—let those soulless bastards take Little Red." He lowered his voice to a whisper as he glanced at Josie's fiery curls. "I know I only saw you with her father from across the ballroom, but he was clearly bad news."

It had been obvious to anyone with eyes and ears what kind of night she and her husband had been having. Bryce hadn't bothered trying to catch up with her about old times; he'd simply waited until Christopher went to the restroom to say hi and give her his number. She'd called Bryce for moral support after she and Josie had moved into an apartment. Shame welled inside her, humiliation that it had taken her so long to admit her husband would never change. Her old friend had seen

Christopher's true colors in a single evening. Why had it taken her years?

In her defense, Bryce had only witnessed her husband drunk and antagonistic. He hadn't seen the determined charmer who'd pursued her or doted on her during their first blissful year of marriage. Plus, Bryce had been looking through the eyes of an adult, not the eyes of a young woman who'd grown up in the foster care system and felt cherished for the first time in her life.

"Chris had his moments," she said softly. She liked to think that some of her late husband's good qualities would live on in Josie.

Bryce waved a hand. "My point was, you make his parents sound about a thousand times worse than him."

"Agreed. But running was a mistake." All she'd ever wanted growing up was a family of her own, yet now she'd endangered her daughter's chances of a normal home life. Josie was still reeling from losing her father. How could she be expected to cope if Heather's impulsive actions landed her in jail? After her arguments with Christopher about operating outside the rules, her failure to appear made her a terrible hypocrite.

"You're not thinking about going back?" Bryce asked dubiously.

Dread knotted her stomach. Her in-laws had scared the hell out of her from the day she'd met them. At first, it had been because she hadn't believed she was good enough for their son—an opinion Eileen Hargrove reinforced at every opportunity. But over the past few years, she'd become apprehensive for other reasons. Christo-

pher had joked that Hargroves were "above the law...
because we can afford to be." Though Heather lacked
specific details, she knew her father-in-law's criminal
activities weren't limited to bribing his way out of traffic tickets.

Not that I can prove it.

"I can't go back," she finally said. "They have unlim-
ited funds and a lawyer who makes great white sharks
look cuddly in comparison." From things she'd overheard during her marriage, Phillip Hargrove might also
have judges and state officials in his back pocket.

"You mentioned funds." Bryce peered at her through
his wire-rim glasses, his concern unmistakable. "Need
a loan?"

She rose, crossing to the expensive ottoman to hug
him. "You are a prince. Why couldn't I have fallen for
you in college?" She'd been nineteen and vastly inex-
perienced with men when she'd met Christopher at a
museum near campus.

"A diligent scholarship student like you with a wast-
rel like me? Pshaw. You couldn't have been expected
to put up with this." He gestured toward the cluttered
tabletop and the magazines now scattered haphazardly
on the unvacuumed carpet. "It would be an affront to
your artistic sensibilities. Now stop trying to change the
subject, and tell me if you need money."

"No. At least, not yet. If I'm careful." When she'd
first considered leaving Christopher, she'd begun quietly squirreling away cash. It had taken her a long time
to work up the courage. She'd later supplemented her

new bank account by selling jewelry. She'd realized she might have to pay for a contentious divorce, but at the end of the day, despite his faults, she'd known Christopher loved Josie. She'd prayed that would guide him to some reasonable decisions.

Eileen and Phillip Hargrove didn't love anyone. They saw Josie, the only child of their only child, as the Hargrove heir, belonging to them by rights—as much a possession as Eileen's BMW or Phillip's Jag.

"What I need—" Heather sighed "—is a *plan*. Other than hauling ass toward the Mexican border."

"With customs security checkpoints? Definitely not the direction you want to head if there's possibly a warrant out for you." His forehead crinkled in concentration. "I might know a place you can go. Ever been to the hill country? I have a cousin in Fredericksburg."

"It's bad enough I imposed on you," she said, not following his train of thought. "I can't show up on your cousin's doorstep."

"You can if she's not home." He was starting to look excited, gesturing with his hands as he spoke. "My cousin Kelsey is married to a guy in the military. He's been overseas a lot but now he's got a six-month assignment in Alaska. She's going to join him, and I arranged for a friend to house-sit. All the regular bills are set for automatic drafts out of Kelsey's bank account. As long as you've got cash for stuff like groceries, you and Little Red would be set. It's perfect!"

"I don't understand. What about your friend who already agreed to do it?"

"She'll be inconvenienced when I tell her Kelsey's changed her mind. And a little peeved," he admitted. "But I'll make sure she lands on her feet. You have a hell of a lot more at stake, Heather."

She was all too aware of the high stakes. To keep the panic at bay, she tried to lighten the moment. "Heather, huh? I think that's the first time you've ever called me anything but 'Red.'"

"About that." He tilted his head, considering. "You stand out with that hair color. Ever thought about going brunette?"

She pressed her fingertips to her eyes. "Not until just now. I'm new at this whole fugitive thing."

"Different hair would help. So would different names. I can assist you there."

She glanced up, startled. "There's a limit to what I'll let you do for me." Even as she said the words, she prayed they were true. How much risk would she let a friend take if it meant protecting her daughter?

"I didn't mean like create new social security numbers for you or falsify a passport," he clarified. "This isn't a Bourne movie. But I might know someone who, uh, dabbles in fake IDs. It would have an upcoming expiration date because the new ones are too hard to copy and it probably wouldn't fool a professional beyond a quick glimpse, but it's a start."

Counterfeit identification and lying about who she was? Bryce's intentions were good, but did she dare continue on this path? Then again… She cast one more anxious glance in Josie's direction. How could she dare *not* take Bryce's help?

Chapter Two

"You haven't said anything since we left the steak house." *Stupid.* Since when was Sergeant Zane Winchester reduced to stating the obvious? His razor-sharp instincts had helped solve cold cases and take down crooked politicians. Colleagues sought his input because he was known for having a quick mind, but a few hours in his teenage daughter's company made him feel like an inept rookie fumbling with a gun for the first time, capable of shooting himself in the foot with one stray word.

Eden glared from the passenger seat of the truck. "What do you want me to say? Thanks for ruining the first nice time I was having since I got shipped to this godforsaken town?"

There were so many things wrong with her retort that he didn't know where to begin. *My fault. Too out of practice.* He hadn't tried hard enough to keep a close bond with her while she and his ex, Valerie, lived in California. Eden didn't let an hour pass without reminding him that she hated her parents' decision to relocate her.

She saw her mother as selfish for ditching her, and she clearly viewed Zane more as prison warden than father.

"What exactly did I do?" Zane asked, trying to better understand the daughter he no longer knew.

"You practically threatened that cute waiter at lunch! You might as well have pulled your gun on him."

"You're exaggerating by a mile. And that 'cute waiter' was too old to be flirting with my fifteen-year-old daughter." He steered onto their street. "You may think you're an adult, Eden Jo, but you're not. Adults face the consequences of their actions. You blame your mama for sending you here, but you refuse to take responsibility for your part in forcing her hand."

"Why are you defending her?" To Eden's credit, she sounded genuinely baffled rather than sarcastic. "You should be mad, too. You didn't want me here."

"That's not true!" Rather than take the time to pull into the garage, he angled crookedly in their driveway and cut the engine so he could focus on her. He studied her face, marveling at the changes. This wasn't the little girl with blond pigtails he used to carry on his shoulders. She was a young woman now, with two thin streaks of hot pink framing her face.

Strips of neon aside, she looked so much like Valerie that he couldn't help a twinge of nervous déjà vu. As a teenager, Val had been beautiful, fascinating and self-destructive. He prayed the similarities between mother and daughter would prove superficial.

He put a hand on Eden's shoulder, an awkward substitution for a hug. "I love you. Even if I'm not crazy about the behavior that led you here, I'm glad to have this time with you."

Her green eyes glittered. "Yeah, I can tell how much you care by all those visits to California and the dozens of phone conversations we had." She wrenched open her door and hopped to the pavement.

He followed, still trying to frame his explanation as he unlocked the front door. On the other side, the dog was already going nuts, barking in manic greeting.

It had hurt like hell to let go of his daughter, but he'd thought it best. When he and Val had divorced, Eden had been just starting that tumultuous journey from adolescence to physical maturity. He'd known there would be questions and scenarios she'd be embarrassed to discuss with him. Instead of an acrimonious custody battle that would compound the pain of the divorce, he'd let Val take her. As Val had reminded him, at least she was around for their daughter, rather than chasing bad guys all across the state of Texas.

With Eden's displeasure filling the foyer, it seemed even colder in the house than it had out in the brisk March breeze. "I never would have given up custody so easily if I hadn't believed it was in your best interest. I figured you'd be better—"

"I *was* better off in California," she interrupted. "If you really loved me, you'd let me go back to my friends and my life there!" Tears spilling from her eyes, she stalked down the hall to the guest room. A moment later, the little ranch-style house shook with the force of her slammed door.

He shifted his weight, torn between the urge to go hug her and the urge to reprimand her for the temperamental display. At the rate she was going, he'd have to replace all the hinges in the house by the time she went back to school on Monday.

"I need some air," he told the dog, a black border collie and shepherd mix splotched with white and gold. "Want to go for a walk?"

Grabbing the leash that hung on a nearby Peg-Board, he called out, "Eden, I'm taking Dolly for a walk around the neighborhood." Unsurprisingly, there was no answer.

Zane hesitated. Was it better to intrude, to hammer home the fact that he was here for her, or should he give her space to adjust to their new arrangement? He wasn't used to feeling conflicted. In years past, Zane and his ex-wife had argued about his "rigid" black-and-white worldview, but having a teenager in the house certainly challenged that perspective. Throwing tantrums and slamming doors were inexcusable for a fifteen-year-old, yet it was difficult to fault Eden's behavior when he was so ashamed of his own. As a father, it had been his responsibility to stay involved in her life, no matter how many miles separated them.

A couple of years ago, when Eden had asked to skip visiting Fredericksburg for the summer because she wanted to attend camp with her friends, he'd agreed instantly. He'd been mired in task force duties as the Rangers sought to shut down a cartel whose members kept slipping across the border. The following June,

Eden had stayed in California because her uncharacteristic dip in grades necessitated summer school. He'd seen her for a few days at Christmas, but awkwardly exchanging presents before sticking her back on a plane wasn't real parenting.

With a sigh, he hooked the leash on Dolly's harness and stepped outside. After only two weeks, Zane was feeling as weary as Val had sounded on the phone.

"I don't know what's wrong with her," his ex-wife had complained. "Maybe she's acting out because she wants your attention. Or maybe I just suck as a role model. But the way she's been behaving, these kids she's been hanging out with…" Her voice had quivered with maternal fear. "You've gotta fix her, Zane. Before she lands in real trouble."

Could he do it? He'd spent a chunk of his life trying to "fix" Val, to no avail. The day he'd signed his divorce papers, he swore he'd learned his lesson. No more rehabilitation attempts thinly disguised as romance. If he ever got involved with a woman again, it had to be as equals. He didn't want to be anyone's life coach or shining knight. The only rescues he'd perform would be in his professional life—a philosophy he'd stuck by, with the exception of Dolly.

After a few weeks of steady meals and belly rubs, Dolly had idolized him. Repairing his relationship with Eden would be far more complicated.

"Doggy!"

Zane glanced up and saw a little girl shoot out of the house next to his. Probably no older than four or five, she looked like a walking accessories department. Her pink shirt and sweatpants were nondescript, but she'd worn them with a sequined scarf and sparkly plastic high heels. The yellow sunglasses dominating her face were so large they made him think of circus clowns. A tiara perched crookedly on her red-gold curls, its fake gemstones sparkling in the sun; clip-on earrings dangled from her lobes, and a feather-trimmed purse hung from her forearm. Peeking out of it was a plastic Tyrannosaurus rex whose snarling expression and sharp teeth were incongruous with her rather exuberant glamour.

He paused, overcome with nostalgia. It seemed only yesterday Eden had been in the throes of her sparkly princess phase. Yet now she was a sullen stranger who stood as tall as his shoulder. The T-rex-toting girl wobbled on her dress-up shoes, then went down with a splat in her front yard.

Shushing Dolly's frenetic woofing, he hurried toward the kid. "Are you okay?"

Her bottom lip trembled. Patches of mud covered her knees. "Ow!"

Previous parenting experience had taught him that sometimes too much sympathy reminded the child she was in pain, while matter-of-fact conversation could work as a distraction. He reeled in Dolly's retractable leash to keep her from licking the girl's face. "Why do you carry a dinosaur in your purse?"

"It's a dog, but you hafta use your imagination. My chihuahua got ripped." The way she said the word, it came out "chowawowa." She sniffled. "Mommy's gonna fix her but she's been too busy with other sewing."

He helped the little girl to her feet. "So, why do you carry a chihuahua in your purse?"

"Because I'm fabulous." She punctuated her statement with an exasperated *duh* look.

"Get your hands off my daughter!" A dark-haired woman flew through the open door at such high speed that he half expected her to face-plant on the lawn, too. She snatched the girl into a protective hug against her body.

The child wiggled, either in embarrassment or protest at her mother's grip. Zane had the absent thought that the freckles smattering the woman's cheeks seemed out of place, too sweet and potentially girlish for someone who'd barreled down on him like an avenging angel.

He took a step back, murmuring softly to Dolly, whose hackles had risen at the woman's shrill approach. "Ma'am, I was just checking to make sure she wasn't hurt when she fell. Zane Winchester." He tipped his white cowboy hat in greeting. "I live next door. You must be the lady Kelsey and Dave got to house-sit?"

She cast him a fleeting glance before returning her attention to the little girl. "You scared me, Belle. What are you doing outside? Never, *never* open the door without me! I told you we'd play in the yard after I went to the bathroom. And after you changed shoes."

The girl's eyes, which were the same golden-brown as her mother's, grew wider and wider, then filled with belated tears. Her left leg buckled dramatically as if she were in too much pain to stand. Zane tried to suppress his grin. *And the award for best actress under ten goes to...*

"I hurt my leg, Mommy."

"Leaving the house without an adult, you're lucky you weren't hurt much worse!" The woman plunged a hand through her short hair, let out an aggrieved sigh, then turned back to Zane. "I suppose I should apologize for snapping your head off."

"You were worried about your child and don't know me," he said. "I'm a parent myself. I get it." She was new to the area, surrounded by strangers—he'd been in California collecting his daughter when the brunette had moved in two weekends ago. Maybe she'd lived in a bad neighborhood before this. It would certainly explain her eyeing him as if he were a convicted criminal.

She tugged on her daughter's arm. "We should get you cleaned up."

"Then can we blow bubbles?" Belle negotiated. "We've been inside *all* day. It's boring!"

"Maybe. In the backyard."

"I still haven't pet the doggy," Belle said pitifully. "What's his name?"

"She's a girl," Zane said. He should walk away. It would be easier for Belle's mama to coax the child inside without the temptation of the dog. But he found himself curious about his new neighbors. "Her name's Dolly."

"Dolly? That doesn't sound like a dog name."

"Tell me about it," he commiserated. "I'd feel a lot less silly yelling something like 'Scout' across the dog park. But I found her while I was doing cleanup after Hurricane Dolly and started calling her that before I realized I was keeping her." In a lot of ways, it had been fitting to name her after a natural disaster. Only a puppy back in 2008, she'd done some significant damage to his belongings in the first few months he'd owned her.

"Change her name," Belle instructed as she patted Dolly on the head. "That's what me and Mommy did."

He frowned, puzzled. "You changed your pet's name?"

At the same time Belle informed him in tragic tones that she did not have a pet, her mother stammered, "N-nicknames. She means nicknames! Belle is short for Isabelle and I go by Alex instead of Alexandra. Alex Hunt."

"I'm Zane," he repeated. "Nice to meet you." He held out his hand, but it took her a moment before she shook it, watching him warily the entire time. She was a stark change from bubbly Kelsey.

Alex raised her gaze, starting to say something, but then she froze like a possum in oncoming headlights.

"Ms. Hunt? Everything okay?"

She eyed the encircled silver star pinned to his denim button-down shirt. He'd been working this morning and hadn't bothered to remove the badge. "Interesting symbol," she said slowly.

"Represents the Texas Rangers."

"Like the baseball team?"

"No, ma'am. Like the law enforcement agency." Maybe that would make her feel safer about her temporary home. He jerked his thumb toward his house. "You have a bona fide lawman living right next door."

Beneath the freckles, her face went whiter than his hat. "Really? That's…" She gave herself a quick shake. "Come on, Belle. Inside now. Before, um, before that mud stains."

"Okay." Belle hung her head but rallied long enough to add, "Bye, Mister Zane. I hope I get to pet Dolly again soon."

From Alex's behavior, Zane had a suspicion they wouldn't be getting together for neighborly potluck dinners anytime in the near future. Instead of commenting on the kid's likelihood of seeing Dolly again, he waved. "Bye, Belle. Stay fabulous."

She beamed. "I will!"

Then mother and daughter disappeared into the house, the front door banging shut behind them.

"Is there something about me," he asked Dolly, "that makes females want to slam doors?"

The only response he got from the dog was an impatient tug on her leash. "Right. I promised you a walk." They started again down the sidewalk, but he found himself periodically glancing over his shoulder and pondering his new neighbors. Cute kid, but she seemed like a handful. And Alex Hunt, once she'd calmed from her mama-bear fury, was perhaps the most skittish woman he'd ever met. If she were a horse, she'd have to wear blinders to keep from jumping at her own shadow. Zane wondered if there was a Mr. Hunt in the picture.

Not that it mattered. The Hunts would only be here

for a matter of months, and he had more pressing priorities than getting to know them. He didn't have the time or energy to win over a nervous neighbor. He still had to figure out how to win over his daughter.

A RANGER. ALEX LEANED against the closed door for support, her palm pressed to her racing heart.

Plenty of women would experience an increase in their pulses at the sight of Zane's green eyes and coal-black hair, but she was more concerned with his occupation than his chiseled cheekbones or broad shoulders. *An honest-to-God, badge-wearing, gun-toting, sworn-to-uphold-the-law Texas freaking Ranger!* Bryce had neglected to mention that.

Josie, without a shy bone in her body—or any concern for the expensive area rug that didn't belong to them—plopped right down in the entryway and began stripping off her muddy leggings. Not Josie, Alex reminded herself. *Belle.* If she was going to keep from blowing their covers, the new names had to be all the time, even in her own thoughts. Otherwise, someone was going to address her as Alex in public and she was going to forget they meant her.

"Belle" happened to be the name of her daughter's favorite Disney princess. She'd seen the movie for the first time last month and had watched the DVD approximately six hundred times since then. Making the switch to the new name had been easy enough, especially once Alex explained that Belle meant beautiful. Her little girl had liked that, even if she hadn't understood why she had to commit to a single new name and couldn't keep changing it every week.

Alex's alias had been chosen for her. When Bryce had handed her the ID, she'd been so fixated on how odd she looked in the picture—her hair dyed espresso with auburn highlights and cropped in a sleek bob that hugged her jawline—that it had taken a moment for the name to even register. She'd told Bryce to surprise her, paranoid that anything she picked would subconsciously hold meaning for her and somehow provide a lead for an astute private investigator.

"Alexandra Hunt?" she'd read, trying to imagine herself as an Alexandra. It seemed too exotic and sophisticated for a single mom whose life consisted of more macaroni than martinis. Then again, being a fugitive was pretty exotic.

Bryce's face had reddened. "She was a character from an old video game, one of the first that got me hooked on gaming. I had kind of a cyber crush on her."

"You named me for a character?" she'd shrieked. "Bryce, anonymity is our goal here! Why not just send me out into the world calling me Lara Croft?"

He'd been unfazed by her anxiety. "Okay, first, there could be lots of civilians who coincidentally have that name. Secondly, no one's going to make the connection. This wasn't a bestselling game. The ideas were solid, but the packaging and distribution…" Then he'd gone on a tangent about software platforms and market shares.

"Mommy?" Belle stood naked, hands on her hips. Alex had been too lost in thought to realize her daughter hadn't stopped with the muddy pants. "Since I got dirty outside, don't you think I should take a bath? Do we have any more of those crayons?"

The sudden attention to hygiene was an obvious ploy to pull out her favorite tub toys and splash around, but Alex was all in favor of that plan. Though she knew she couldn't keep her daughter housebound for the next five and a half months, she didn't like the idea of Belle hanging out in the yard, within easy conversational distance of the lawman next door.

"A bath sounds like a great idea," Alex said. Maybe she'd treat herself to a similar luxury tonight—a long hot bubble bath after Belle was asleep and the doors were securely locked. She still couldn't believe her daughter had taken advantage of the few minutes Alex had been in the bathroom to bolt out the front door, but dogs were a powerful enticement to the little girl. Belle's fifth birthday was next month; the only present she'd asked for was a puppy.

That's all I need. Then I'd be a fugitive on the lam with my fugitive princess daughter and our fugitive dog. A bubble of hysteria rose in her throat.

"Mommy? Why are you laughing?"

"No reason, punkin. Come on, let's get you clean again."

She followed her daughter upstairs to the bathroom, where Belle's hot pink towel hung alongside the more color-coordinated linens belonging to the home's owners. It was surreal to be here, surrounded by someone else's furniture, someone else's keepsakes, someone else's wedding picture hanging on the wall. Everything was foreign. Between the unfamiliar setting, the ugly used car she'd given Bryce cash to purchase, the new hair and the new name, Alex hardly knew who she was anymore.

I'm a mother. And I have a daughter to keep safe.

Everything else—including her nausea over lying to a law enforcement officer and the terror that she might get caught—was unimportant.

Chapter Three

As soon as Eden rounded the corner to the ladies' room, Zane turned to Officer Ben Torres. "I'm sorry." The words caught unpleasantly in Zane's throat. Having to apologize for his daughter stung. He wished others could see the sunny, sweet girl he remembered. "We've been lousy company tonight."

Ben, a Fredericksburg police officer, was recovering from an on-duty injury. When the two men had talked on Monday, Ben had mentioned that he had a doctor's appointment on Wednesday and was scheduled to graduate from a wheelchair to crutches. Since he'd received the medical okay this morning, Zane had offered to buy him dinner in celebration. Ben had suggested the Torres family restaurant where he ate for free, assuring Zane it was the thought that counted. Zane hadn't cared where they ate as long as it got him out of the house. The strained suppers at home, with Eden barely responding to questions about her new high school, were taking its toll. Especially after yesterday's call from the guidance counselor that she was using her midsemester move as an excuse for not doing homework, claiming that she was still trying to catch up and that her workload was daunting. Zane knew his daughter, a former honors student, was capable of far more when she applied herself. He was angry, but he hadn't meant to inflict their prickly relationship on innocent bystanders.

"Don't worry about me," Ben said. "I'm growing accustomed to lousy company. My brother's been living with me since he and his wife separated. He was always a serious guy, but now he's downright grim. Next to him, Eden's full of bubbly cheer."

"She used to be. There was a time…" Zane trailed off uncomfortably, not in the habit of discussing personal matters.

Recalling Eden's childhood exuberance reminded him of the spirited girl who'd accosted him and Dolly over the weekend. Instinct told him Belle Hunt didn't have a father in the immediate picture. For one thing, Kelsey had said she was leaving the care of her house to a lady, not a family. Had Alexandra Hunt needed a place to get back on her feet after her marriage fell apart? He silently wished her luck—single parenting wasn't for wimps.

He ground his teeth. "Do you think all children of divorced parents turn bitter?"

"Divorce is tough, but you're oversimplifying," Ben chided. "Don't you think it's difficult for a teen to change schools midyear and make new friends no matter what her parents' marital status? Besides, moodiness is normal for teenage girls. I grew up with a sister, remember?" He contorted his face into a comical mask of horror.

"Oh, please. Grace is one of the most hospitable people I've ever met!"

The three Torres siblings jointly owned The Twisted Jalapeño, but Chef Grace Torres was the one who ran the restaurant.

Ben rolled his eyes. "Sure, she's the soul of hospitality now, as an adult trying to drum up repeat business for this place, but you should have seen her at fourteen! Maybe what Eden needs is a woman who can relate to her. Too bad your last date was back when dinosaurs were leaving those footprints in the Hondo Creek bed."

"I haven't noticed anyone special in your life, either," Zane grumbled. Although he *had* noticed Ben sneaking surreptitious glances toward Amy Winthrop, the bartender. "Speaking of women, do you know anything about Alex Hunt? She's living next to me temporarily, house-sitting for Kelsey and Dave Comer."

"We should ask Grace." Ben nodded at his crutches. "I haven't exactly been man about town lately. Thank God the festival starts this weekend. I'm going stir-crazy."

Frederick-Fest was a weeklong annual tradition that attracted tourists from all over the state and vendors from all over the country. Zane would be working some shifts to assist with security and crowd control.

"Will you be mobile enough to volunteer at the festival?" Zane asked.

"Not in my usual capacity, but I can work the first

aid booth when other people need a lunch break. And Amy and I are going to sit at a table handing out promotional stuff for the restaurant."

"Ah." Zane smirked. "The lovely Amy."

"Who's Amy?"

Both men started as Eden slid back into her chair. Apparently she'd killed as much time as she possibly could in the restroom by braiding her blond hair and applying far too much makeup.

Zane did a double take. "Any particular reason you're trying to make yourself look like a raccoon?"

Slashes of red appeared on her cheeks, and he regretted his words. He didn't approve of the pound of cosmetics she'd slathered on her face, but he shouldn't embarrass her in front of Ben. He was grateful when Ben answered her question, heading off any sarcastic retort.

"Amy is my sister's roommate. She works here." He gestured toward the bar and waved.

A pretty woman with purple-tinted hair waved back, making Zane ashamed of his knee-jerk reaction. Amy, with her tattoo and the line of earrings adorning her ear, was kindhearted and responsible. Maybe he shouldn't let a couple of pink streaks in Eden's hair and her enthusiastic use of eyeliner bother him so much.

"I was just telling your dad," Ben continued, "that Amy and I will be working a shift at the festival. It starts this weekend."

"Yeah, I heard some kids in class talking about a festival." Eden sounded intrigued.

"We used to go every year as a family," Zane said. "You remember the pony rides and all the food? I used to dance with you."

"Ew." Eden's grimace made it clear she would not welcome a dance with her father at the polka pavilion.

Their waiter appeared, plates of hot entrées lined up his arm in such a seemingly precarious way that it was a miracle he hadn't dropped everything on his walk from the kitchen.

"You're going to love the food," Ben promised. He'd expressed surprise when he'd learned this was Eden's first visit to the Jalapeño, admonishing Zane that two and a half weeks was far too long a wait.

Ben's words proved prophetic. After the first few bites, Eden wolfed down her food with the gusto and appetite Zane remembered from his own teenage years—when his mother used to tease that he couldn't come grocery shopping with her because he'd eat half the purchases in the car before she could get them home. Between Eden's enjoyment of the food and periodic questions about the festival, it was the most animated Zane had seen her since her arrival.

God bless the Torres family, he found himself thinking at the end of the evening. Chef Grace Torres had come to their table to say hi and make sure everything was delicious, and Eden had seemed a little starstruck to meet someone who was going to appear on a reality show.

Grace had explained that the producers wanted to film the cooking competition during the festival. "When the first episode airs, Amy and I are going to host a viewing party. You and your dad will have to come. Unless of course I lose. In which case, I plan to hibernate for a year in the longest pity party Gillespie County has ever seen."

"There's no way you can lose," Eden had protested. "Your food is awesome!"

But once they were in the truck after dinner, Zane was on his own again, without Ben or Grace to ride to his rescue. "Glad you liked dinner," he told his daughter. "We'll have to eat there more often."

Eden nodded promptly—confirming that the Jalapeño was the first thing she officially liked about Fredericksburg—but remained quiet.

He cleared his throat. "I, uh…I shouldn't have said you look like a raccoon."

She flinched, which wasn't the reaction he'd hoped to get.

"I have to be at the festival most of the weekend," he said. "Want to come with me and check it out?" When she shrugged noncommittally, he played the ace up his sleeve. "Ben mentioned the other day that Grace and the other contestants on that reality show will be doing some live demonstrations. You want an in-person sneak peek? Who knows—if the camera crew pans the audience, maybe you'll end up on TV, too."

She swiveled in her seat. "You think so? That would be awesome."

"I don't see why not. It happens at sporting events all the time. The producers might even interview people to get their opinion on the food. If there's one thing the festival has plenty of, it's food."

"What about rides?" Eden asked. "I love roller coasters."

"Well, there aren't any big coasters, but there are some carnival rides." He was giving her a rundown of attractions and scheduled events when they pulled up in front of the house.

Eden was engaged enough in the conversation that when he walked down the driveway to get the mail, she came with him rather than disappear into the house. A high-pitched "Hey, Mister Zane!" caused them both to turn at the same time.

In the driveway next door, Belle and her mother were walking toward their beater of a car. The vehicle was easily older than Eden. Hell, it might be older than him.

Even in the dim illumination provided by the streetlight, he could see Alex scowl. Now that he'd had time to mull it over, he was almost certain she was going through a divorce. Maybe she was at that stage where she disliked all men. It was a more palatable explanation than her hating him personally, for no discernible reason.

"Hey, Belle," he called back, not breaking stride as he proceeded to the mailbox. The Hunts were obviously on their way out, and he didn't plan to intrude on Alex's evening.

"Who's the cute little kid?" Eden asked.

"Temporary neighbors, house-sitting for the people who live there. They moved in about the same time you got here." Too bad Belle wasn't a decade older. Then maybe she and Eden could commiserate about both being new girls.

Eden seemed unbothered by the age difference, though. She was already walking toward the other two females. "Hi," she chirped. "I'm Eden Winchester. I like your crown!"

Belle wore yet another tiara—this one paired with a feather boa. She preened at Eden's compliment, but then frowned. "Did you get hit in the face? I saw a movie where a bad guy got hit and his eye looked like that. But it was just one, not both."

Alex slapped a palm to her forehead. "That's not nice, Belle."

"I didn't get punched," Eden said. "It's makeup."

"Oh!" Belle brightened. "I love makeup. I have a whole kit. Nail polish and lipstick and skin glitter. You should play makeup with me, and I'll show you how. Yours looks funny."

"Like a raccoon?" Eden flashed a grin over her shoulder, and Zane's heart squeezed in his chest. He felt as if he and his daughter shared a joke, as if they were finally a team rather than two opposing sides. Her smile bought years of memories cascading back. *That's the Eden I know.*

He ambled toward the three women, suddenly loath to let the Hunts get away. "Where are you ladies headed?"

"The store," Belle announced. "Mommy forgot dinner."

"I didn't forget," Alex insisted. "I made a pot of

homemade sauce, and it's been simmering for hours. I just didn't realize we had no spaghetti. I'm still not used to living out of someone else's pantry. At home, noodles are a staple."

Zane wondered where "home" was. "I think I have spaghetti. Why don't you come over, and we can check?"

She actually retreated, bumping into the side of her car. He was half-surprised the door didn't fall off the ancient sedan. Surely her former home was within a few hours' drive. That clunker wouldn't have made it far.

"Oh, no," Alex said in a rush. "Belle and I don't want to impose."

Her daughter had other ideas. "Yay! Can I pet Dolly? Come on, Mommy." She raced into the Winchesters' driveway, telling Eden, "I met Dolly the other yesterday. She likes me!"

Eden nodded, her voice a pseudo-whisper. "Dolly has very good taste. She only likes the most special people."

And the most "fabulous," Zane thought with an inward smile. Perhaps he should feel guilty about their ganging up on Alex. She looked like she'd rather drink strychnine than investigate the contents of his kitchen, but after all, he was trying to do the woman a favor. She and Belle were probably starving. Why drive all the way to the grocery store?

"It's no imposition," Zane assured her. He gazed pointedly to the girls, who had linked hands, and lowered his voice. "Don't look now, but I think you're outvoted."

"Are you going to the festival?" Eden asked Belle.

The little girl's forehead puckered. "What's a festival?"

"It's a fair. There will be rides and performing animals and games to play."

"I like animals!" Belle turned wide eyes on her mother, imploring, "Please? It sounds fun! I never get any fun."

Eden tousled the girl's hair, knocking the tiara askew. "You, either, huh?"

"One thing at a time," Alex said, a thread of desperation in her voice. "Let's worry about getting some dinner into you. We'll talk about the festival later."

"So you'll accept the offer to raid my pantry?" Zane pressed.

"Doesn't look like I have much choice."

It wasn't the most gracious thank-you he'd ever received, but luckily for Alex, he'd had a lot of recent practice with a grudging female. After a couple of weeks of Eden's attitude, his neighbor's surliness bounced right off him. As they approached his lawn, they could hear Dolly barking inside the house. Belle ran on ahead as if she could somehow get through the locked door.

Eden hung back long enough to confide, "I always wanted a kid sister. But an adorable neighbor is good for now." Then she caught up to Belle, leaving her father startled.

He'd never thought about whether Eden wanted siblings or not. Both he and Valerie had been only children, so it had seemed natural to have just one. Besides, he and Valerie hadn't shared a bed much in the final years of their marriage, not after he'd caught her sharing other men's.

Alex walked beside him, her stiff body language screaming her reluctance. "I'm guessing there's no wife at home to resent our intrusion?"

He shook his head. "Divorced single parent. You?"

She was silent for a long minute, and he watched her gnaw at her bottom lip. Finally, in a tone so soft it was barely audible, she said, "Widowed. Since last spring."

Her answer hit him with tangible force. He'd been so sure she was divorced or separated. It had never occurred to him Belle's father might be dead.

"I'm so sorry," he said.

"I…apologize if I haven't seemed very neighborly. It's been hard." She gave a quick, brittle laugh. "Understatement."

"Well, if there's anything I can do," he offered. "Spaghetti noodles. Car maintenance."

"That's kind of you, Mr. Winchester, but Belle and I have to learn to stand on our own feet."

"An admirable sentiment." He crossed to his porch and unlocked the front door. Dolly practically knocked him down in her excitement.

Eden grabbed the dog by the collar. "Belle and I will take her out back."

He motioned for Alex to come inside. "After you." He couldn't help noticing how she tried to shrink her body as she passed him, flattening herself against the doorjamb to insure they wouldn't accidentally touch.

Though she clearly wasn't comfortable around him

yet, maybe they could help each other. She was new in town and might need a tour guide of sorts. Their daughters had certainly hit it off; he'd never seen Eden warm to someone so instantaneously. Alex Hunt might not think she was in the right state of mind to make new friends, but Zane resolved to prove her wrong. That smile Eden had flashed him when she made the raccoon remark still warmed him from the inside, like hot chocolate.

I'm not a bad guy, he silently promised Alex. *And I think you'll grow to like me.* He hoped so, anyway.

Because if he had anything to do with it, their families would definitely be spending time together.

Chapter Four

Alex waited while Tess Fitzpatrick, a local dance teacher, counted out bills from the petty cash drawer. Tess was a cheerful redhead with a round face and pert features that made her look younger than she was. The first time Alex had come into the studio, she'd hesitated, not sure if Tess worked here or was a teenage student.

"We are so lucky you answered our ad," Tess said as she handed Alex an envelope. "With all of our age groups and classes performing at the festival, we really need the extra help with costumes and sets."

Last week, Alex had seen the notice for a seamstress who could alter ballet costumes that didn't quite fit and do minor repairs on older pieces from the studio's wardrobe closet. Alex had learned to sew early in life, often refurbishing or embellishing ill-fitting hand-me-downs so she wouldn't feel like such a loser wearing them.

She returned Tess's smile. "I'm happy to lend a hand—especially since you're paying me."

"Only a nominal amount," Tess fretted. "As skilled as you are, you should be better compensated."

"I'm not complaining. I'm just glad you didn't mind

paying me in cash." She'd rather not tempt fate by trying to cash checks made out to "Alexandra Hunt."

Alex had stammered through a clumsy explanation
about her bank not having local branches and how it
wasn't worth starting a new account since her stay here
would only be temporary. Tess was too good-natured to
question the awkward rambling, but Alex knew she was
a terrible liar. Hell, she felt guilty and self-conscious just
standing in the same room with another redhead. Tess's
ginger curls made Alex nervous that her dye job was
blatantly obvious in comparison. Even though Bryce
had assured her she looked great, her new, sleek, dark
hair occasionally made her feel like an actress in a bad
spy film.

If only this *were* a movie and not her real life! Tension knotted her stomach, but she tried to keep her voice
light as she addressed her daughter.

"Come on, punkin." The little girl stood watching
through an interior window into the ballet studio. "Time
to go grocery shopping."

Belle kept her gaze on the dozen six-year-olds who
jumped and spun in a whirl of black leotards and gauzy
pink skirts. "They're pretty," she said wistfully.

Alex was so on edge that she almost jumped when
Tess reached out and cupped her wrist.

"Sorry." Tess's brown eyes were contrite. "I didn't
mean to startle you. I was trying to be discreet." She
glanced in Belle's direction and dropped her voice to
such a hushed whisper that Alex was nearly reduced
to lipreading.

"I don't want to speak out of turn," Tess began. "Although, I am sort of known for that around town. Anyway, I realize you won't be here long and it may not be in your budget, but if she wanted to attend a class, we could work something out. Maybe trade a few more sequin maintenance jobs for—"

"Class? Can I, Mommy? Can I take a class?" Belle's attention was fully on her mother now, the spinning dancers behind the glass forgotten.

Tess winced. "I didn't mean for her to overhear that."

"Don't blame yourself." Alex shot her daughter a reproachful look. "She has bionic hearing or something. I've never understood how she does it."

"Please?" Belle asked.

"That's for me and Miss Fitzpatrick to discuss later. Right now, it's time to buy groceries." Alex herded her daughter toward the door, trying not to think about how many puppies and dance lessons Eileen and Phillip Hargrove could afford. *Yeah, they're loaded, but giving Chris every single thing he ever asked for didn't do him much good, did it?* She couldn't let the Hargroves get their cold hands on her daughter. Even if her suspicions about their criminal tendencies were exaggerated— which she doubted—she knew they were dangerous in other ways.

Belle walked silently to the car, doing nothing to help while Alex buckled her into the booster seat. "Miss our old car," the girl finally grumbled.

Me, too. Alex had insisted Bryce find her something with at least minimal safety features, but she hoped she never had to put any of them to the test. In the event of a collision, the air bags in this piece of junk seemed more likely to whimper in defeat than deploy. She bit her lip, recalling Zane Winchester's unexpected offer last night, when he'd told her he was willing to help with anything from pasta to car maintenance. As a mother, she couldn't help wondering if it would be worth the risk to let him look over the vehicle and make sure it was roadworthy, for Belle's sake. But as a woman on the run, inviting the law over to look under her hood was a really bad idea.

In the backseat, Belle remained uncharacteristically silent. She didn't recover her normal verve until the produce section of the grocery store. She stood next to the cart, bouncing on the balls of her feet as Alex compared fruit prices.

"Mommy, apples are healthy, aren't they?"

Alex picked up a bag of seedless grapes. "Mmm-hmm."

"And exercise is healthy. There was a song about it on my show this morning." With projection a vocal coach would applaud, she belted out, "'Gotta move, *move, MOVE* to find your healthy groove! You gotta—'"

"Shh!" Alex pressed her fingertips to Belle's mouth.

Her daughter squirmed away. "Don't do that."

"Sorry, but you're not supposed to be so loud in the store. They probably have rules about that. We don't want to get in trouble." Not that Belle had any concept of how much trouble they could attract. Was there anyone in the world less suited to lying low and not drawing attention? "No more singing until we get home, okay?"

"Okay." Belle nodded in prompt agreement, a cherubic picture of obedience. "Is dancing exercise?"

Alex sighed, realizing where this exchange had been leading all along. "I said I'd consider the lessons with Miss Tess. I need time to think about it."

Alex's top priority was to keep her daughter hidden and safe. Ballet classes were unnerving. The less Belle interacted with others, the better. But on the other hand, how was the nearly-five-year-old supposed to develop socially and emotionally if her mother kept her isolated in a strange house? Every bit as vivacious as her father had been, Belle needed to be around people.

"Guess what?" Alex changed the subject. "I decided we're going to the festival this weekend." It was a stop-gap measure, one that would make Belle happy without being as risky as regular dance lessons where she might make friends and unwittingly confide in her classmates.

"We *are?*" Belle stretched her arms out and spun in a circle. "They have balloon animals at the festival! Eden said so. And pony rides."

As Alex steered the cart down the bread aisle, Belle kept up a monologue of everything she planned to do and eat at Frederick-Fest. For the first time since they'd showed up in town, Alex felt as if she'd done something right. Maybe the festival would be good for both of them. Lord knew she could use the diversion.

They finished their shopping and progressed to the checkout line, where the cashier took note of the five boxes of spaghetti noodles and smiled. "Having a dinner party?"

Alex's face heated and she didn't bother answering as she paid. She hadn't realized she'd grabbed that many boxes. Had she subconsciously thought that if she armed herself with enough pasta she could avoid running into Zane Winchester again? Unlikely. The man lived next door. It would have been nice if she could park in the Comers' garage, all the better to dodge her neighbors when she was coming and going from the house, but the garage was full.

Full of the Comers' belongings. Because it's their *home.* This house-sitting situation was fortuitous but temporary. Now that she and Belle had settled into a "safe" place long enough to regroup, Alex had to come up with a long term plan to protect her daughter.

In a perfect world, Alex could stay one step ahead and the Hargroves would never find them. But she couldn't count on that. She desperately wished she had ammunition against them, insurance she could use to make them relent. For the sake of her marriage—and because she'd thought it prudent to stay beneath the Hargroves' radar as much as possible—she'd tried for years to ignore her instincts about her parents-in-law. If she'd dug deeper, would she now have enough information to be a real threat to them?

Not necessarily. Even if she'd been brave enough to ask questions sooner, who would have given her straight answers? Besides, if evidence of Phillip Hargrove's corruption was so easy to come by, someone would have used it by now. No matter how many smiling people clapped him on the back at the country club, the man had a few enemies. But Phillip did enough social and financial damage to his opponents to discourage people from acting against him. He wasn't used to being thwarted.

A perverse grin tugged at her lips. The man who didn't tolerate ever being told *no* must have been downright apoplectic when he learned his "mousy nobody" of a daughter-in-law had defied him. She wished she could have seen the look on his face when he'd realized she wasn't walking into that courtroom. Her self-congratulatory moment faded as quickly as it came, though. She'd caught them off guard the first time simply because it had never occurred to them that she would have the gumption to leave, just as Chris had underestimated her ability to walk away from him. Now Eileen and Phillip had a better understanding of the lengths she would go to in order to keep Josie out of their clutches.

Without the element of surprise on her side, what other weapons did she have in her arsenal?

FOLLOWING DINNER THURSDAY night, Zane delegated the job of walking the dog to Eden. "Don't go far. They're predicting a storm tonight. And don't forget to take some baggies with you to clean up after her."

She made a face. "Gross. Come on, Dolly, let's get this over with."

"So you can beat the rain and hurry back to focus on that makeup homework, right?"

He'd found several opportunities during dinner to stress the importance of her grades—and remind her he'd be checking her work from now on to make sure it was complete. At this latest mention, Eden shot him a look that could pierce Kevlar. But she didn't make a surly retort, which was progress. *Maybe I'm getting through to her.*

He'd had a brainstorm at lunch on how to further encourage his daughter to become an upstanding member of society. At the restaurant, Ben had commented that it might benefit Eden to have a woman she could relate to as a role model. Would it also help Eden to be someone else's role model? She'd doted on Belle Hunt. She'd been so patient and good-natured with the little girl; perhaps giving them more time together would motivate Eden to be a sterling example.

He just needed Alex Hunt's cooperation.

Today he'd found himself thinking about the lovely widow far more than he should; the sadness in her eyes haunted him. He wanted to help her smile again. Granted, she'd been a bit skittish in his presence so far, but if she got to know him better… His divorce had been difficult even with friends and his parents nearby to help him through it. He could barely fathom how Alex felt, alone with no local support network. Zane could take her to dinner, officially welcome her to town and let her know he was here for her.

For a second, doubt gripped him—was this another ill-advised attempt at rescuing a damsel in distress?

No. It was simply an invitation to dinner. According to Ben, men issued such invitations to women all the time.

Zane scrawled a quick note saying he'd be back soon and changed into a faded San Antonio Spurs T-shirt with his jeans. Both times he'd interacted with Alex, she'd seemed intimidated. To put her at ease, he wanted to appear as casual and approachable as possible.

About a month ago, when he'd been eating alone at The Twisted Jalapeño, Grace Torres had stopped at his table to tease him about looking stern and hyperalert. "At least three patrons have asked if you're here tonight to take down a criminal," she'd said. "I would take it as a personal favor if you could at least pretend to relax and enjoy my food."

Smile, he reminded himself as he cut across his lawn into the Comers' front yard. *Be friendly*. He wanted to coax Alex into seeing things his way, not scare her. That outdated monstrosity of a car was in the driveway, so he assumed the Hunts were home.

He knocked at the front door, calling "Hello?" for good measure. "It's Zane." He could understand a single woman not wanting to open the door to unexpected visitors after dark.

There were footsteps on the other side, followed by the metallic rattle and click of the chain being unfastened and the dead bolt being unlocked.

Alex greeted him in a resigned tone. "Mr. Winchester. What brings you here?"

Her eyebrows were raised in a quizzical expression. They were a ruddy gold, much closer to the color of Belle's red curls than to Alex's dark hair. Many women liked to experiment with different shades, but he couldn't help wondering how Alex looked with her natural color. Beautiful, he imagined.

She would be beautiful anyway if her features weren't so often pinched with apprehension.

Realizing he'd yet to speak, he gave her a broad smile. *Friendly, approachable.* "I, uh, have something to discuss with you. Can I come in for a second?"

"Hi, Mister Zane!" Belle joined her mother at the door. "Want a hot dog? We're eating dinner."

"I deduced that," he said, trying not to laugh at the little girl's colorful cheeks and chin.

She wrinkled her nose. "What's 'deduce'?"

Alex glanced down at her daughter, the tenderness in her gaze transforming her appearance. "It means using clues to figure something out. The mustard and ketchup all over your face are pretty big clues." She stepped back, allowing Zane inside. "If you're done eating, Belle, go upstairs and wash your face. You can play in your room while Mr. Winchester and I talk."

When Belle frowned, obviously not pleased at being banished, Zane added, "Listen to your mama now." The little girl hesitated, then nodded and scampered up the stairs. At Alex's surprised expression, he said, "Hope I wasn't out of line, telling her what to do. Force of habit."

"From parenting Eden?"

"From the job, actually. In law enforcement, we provide backup for each other."

Alex would do anything for her daughter, but she

had to admit, single parenting could get difficult. On Belle's occasional Holy Terror days, it would be nice to know someone else had her back. Bath times and bedtimes might be easier if she could depend on a partner. *Cover me, I'm going in.*

Zane gave her an expectant smile. "So where can we talk?"

Maybe the reason for his dropping by was as simple as letting her know about a neighborhood garage sale. But her self-preservation instincts wanted to manufacture an excuse to shove him back out the door. This was the first time she'd ever seen him without his omnipresent white hat. His dark hair was appealingly rumpled, and he wore a black T-shirt with jeans. Inexplicably, she found him more dangerous like this than if he'd shown up with a gun and badge. At least the badge was a reminder that she couldn't let her guard down.

"Let's go in the kitchen," she said. "But if you don't want Belle to overhear, it might be easier to pass notes back and forth on a sheet of paper. As I told Tess Fitzpatrick today, my daughter has some sort of sonic superhearing."

"Oh, you know Tess? That's great!" He beamed at her. What was with him tonight? Spokespeople for teeth whitener didn't smile this much. "Making lots of new friends in town?"

Not especially. It was difficult to bond when you were lying about who you were and considered the day a success if you'd managed not to speak to anyone. She went into the kitchen, busying herself with rinsing dirty dishes and loading them into the washer.

He leaned against the island behind her, far too close for her peace of mind. "Anything I can do to help?"

Leave. "No, I've got it." She cringed at the abrupt edge in her voice. "Thanks anyway, Mr. Winchester."

"Zane," he corrected. "I'd like to be on that list of new friends. After all, we're neighbors. Plus, we're in the same boat."

The Texas Ranger and the failure-to-appear outlaw mom? They weren't even in the same ocean.

"With both of us raising girls on our own," Zane said, "you and I have a lot in common. We know how stressful single parenting can be. When was the last time you had a night out, just some adult conversation and a few hours to relax?"

Warning sirens clanged in her head. All his smiling tonight…had he been flirting with her? "Are you asking me on a *date?*" She lost her grip on a slick wet glass. It hit the tile floor and shattered.

Zane swore under his breath. "You're barefoot. Where can I find a broom?"

"Laundry room around the corner," she said, feeling clumsy and foolish. If she didn't want to draw attention to her and Belle, she had to stop overreacting to everything. But the thought of Zane asking her out caused her head to spin.

While she waited, she bent to pick up the largest pieces. She wondered if she could find the Comers a replacement glass that matched the one she'd broken. "Ow!" A drop of blood bloomed on the tip of her finger.

Zane hurried back with a broom and dustpan. "Did you step on a piece?"

She pointed to the large jagged hunk of glass that sat on the counter. "I was getting the biggest pieces out of the way to make sweeping up the shards easier."

He set the broom against the island and reached for her. "Put your arms around my neck."

"What? No, I—"

But he was already lifting her as if she weighed no more than Belle. Alex's heart thudded in erratic tempo. When was the last time a man had held her? Up close, she realized just how green Zane's eyes were. Not blue-green or a diluted hazel, but clear and—

"There you go." He righted her next to the kitchen table and took her hand in his, examining it beneath the Comers' funky chandelier. "I don't see a sliver. First aid supplies?"

She waved her free hand toward the kitchen drawer where she kept Belle's adhesive bandages.

He chuckled when he found them. "You want one printed with polka-dotted puppies or kittens wearing crowns?"

Alex sank into a chair, wishing she could rewind to when she'd first opened the door and do everything differently. *For starters, I wouldn't open the door.* "Surprise me."

He returned a moment later with an adhesive strip and antibiotic ointment.

"Thanks." She didn't meet his eyes as he took her hand. His grip was warm and strong and he was slow to let go of her after he'd bandaged the cut.

"Alex?" His voice was a husky rumble, and she couldn't help wondering how he would sound saying her real name.

She stiffened at the mental slip. *For all intents and purposes, Alex* is *your real name. Keep it together.*

"I didn't mean to make you uncomfortable earlier," he apologized. "I just thought maybe you'd like to have dinner sometime. You're new in town and don't know anyone. And…I'd really like to get to know you."

Their gazes locked. For a moment she desperately wanted to say yes. In addition to being undeniably attractive, Zane seemed like a great guy, straightforward and dependable. Trustworthy. *Unlike me.* She belatedly remembered that it was imperative he *didn't* get to know her, not the real her.

"I can't," she blurted. "Thank you, but no."

"I see." Disappointment clouded his gaze as he turned away. He began sweeping broken glass into the dustpan. "I'm tempted to try to talk you into it anyway, just an evening out as friends, but I was raised to be more chivalrous than that. A gallant man should accept a woman's refusal gracefully."

She steered the subject away from her personal life. "So who instilled this code of chivalry, your mom or dad?"

"Both." His mouth curved in an affectionate smile that seemed more natural than his earlier toothy grins.

"He was a fireman and she was a nurse. They're retired now, living in an apartment at Gunther Gardens, but age doesn't stop them from volunteering around the community. They share a strong drive to help others."

"They sound like good people." It made sense that two civic-minded, everyday heroes had raised a strapping lawman with a penchant for wanting to help.

"What about your parents?" Zane asked. "Are they retired or still working?"

"Don't actually know," she said, her voice tight. "I was a ward of the state."

Was it folly to share that personal fact with him? Did it make her more identifiable, should anyone ever ask about her? Zane didn't need to know she'd been abandoned as a sickly toddler. She'd needed so much extra care that no one had adopted her. Eventually, she'd become as healthy as any other child, but she'd never found a permanent home.

"I don't really like to talk about it," she added. She glanced pointedly at the cheap digital watch that was light-years away from the diamond-studded Cartier Christopher had given her when they'd learned she was pregnant the first time. "Not to be rude, but I need to run Belle's bath soon."

"Right. One quick favor to ask, then I'll go. Would you let Eden babysit for your daughter sometime? If you and Tess ever wanted to go see a movie, for example. I would owe you big-time."

"You would?" Alex blinked, not sure how hiring his daughter to babysit was a favor to him. "Is Eden trying to save up for a car or something?" She knew parents of teens often encouraged their kids to seek employment, but Zane's going door to door on his daughter's behalf seemed a touch overzealous.

"This isn't about money," he said. "It's about responsibility. My ex asked if Eden could come live with me because she'd fallen in with a bad crowd in California, developed some dangerous habits. She was becoming argumentative, disrespectful, sneaky."

"You realize you're not painting a picture of someone I want to entrust with my only child?" she asked wryly.

"She's still a good kid deep down," he maintained, sounding as if he was trying to convince himself as much as Alex. "I catch glimpses of it, like last night. Watching her with Belle was encouraging. She was the Eden I remember, the young woman I believe she can be. There are a lot of rehabilitative programs that focus on giving offenders more responsibility as a way to improve self-worth and behavior."

Damn it. Alex understood too well the need to do what was best for one's child; she empathized with his goal. And after turning down his dinner invitation, saying yes to this seemed like the least she could do. Further entangling her and Belle's life with Zane and his daughter's, however, was too big a gamble to take.

She was slow to answer, trying to frame her refusal gently. "I appreciate your being so candid with me." Didn't she owe him some honesty in return? If she'd stepped on the broken glass, it wouldn't have stung more than her conscience did now. "The truth is, I've always been a little overprotective of my daughter, even before my husband's death. Belle wasn't my first pregnancy. Before her, I...lost two. Then I went into labor with her prematurely. I was terrified. She's my miracle, and I can't let anything happen to her. The idea of letting a teenager I don't know well, one with a history of irresponsibility—"

"I understand," Zane interrupted. "And I won't take up any more of your time."

He looked so dejected that it was on the tip of her tongue to offer a compromise, such as suggesting they discuss this again after she was better acquainted with Eden. But Alex couldn't afford to get any better acquainted with the Winchesters! It was temptingly easy to talk to Zane. In one short conversation, she'd mentioned being a foster child and her miscarriages, both of which were private matters she rarely discussed.

Maybe if he weren't such a good listener, maybe if he weren't a sympathetic fellow single parent or didn't have such intense green eyes, they could have shared a casual friendship. The very attributes that made him so attractive made him nearly as dangerous to her and Belle as the Hargroves.

Chapter Five

After a day and a half of stormy weather, Alex woke on Saturday to early-morning sunshine. She stretched in bed, taking a moment to savor the peace and quiet, then realized that something was obviously wrong. *Like those movies where a commando says "too quiet" right before the ambush.* When was the last time she'd been allowed to wake up naturally? Her daughter, a habitually early riser, should have shaken her awake demanding breakfast or asking if it was time to go the festival yet.

"Belle?" Alex called as she swung her feet out of the bed. "Are you upstairs, honey?" Her daughter knew how to turn on the downstairs television, which stayed tuned to a child-friendly channel. But Belle was not a particularly stealthy child. Even if she'd chosen to forgo breakfast and had suppressed her excitement over the festival, it seemed unlikely she could have tiptoed down the stairs without alerting Alex.

Alex had just stepped into the hall when she heard her daughter's answering moan. She quickened her pace and found Belle curled into a tight ball, her breathing uneven. She looked as if she was holding her stomach beneath the sheets. Belle opened her eyes long enough to grimace in her mom's direction, then closed them again.

"Hey, punkin." Alex sat on the bed, stroking her daughter's hair away from her face. The curls were damp to the touch, and Belle's skin was hot. "Not feeling so good this morning, huh?"

"I'm *not* sick," Belle said angrily. "Today's the festival."

Alex's heart sank in disappointment for her little girl. But there was a bright side here. "It's a weeklong event. We have lots of chances to go." A lot of the local businesses were operating on a shortened schedule for the next week, and school kids were getting out at noon.

"But we were gonna go today!"

Alex thought it best not to further upset her daughter by arguing. "I need to get you medicine for your fever. Then you can get some more rest, and we'll talk about it after you wake up."

Belle sat bolt upright, but immediately slumped as if she'd used her last reserve of energy. "If I take the medicine, I can go?"

"I'm not making any promises about today. The most important thing is getting you all better. Do you want some juice? Or a cold washcloth?"

"No. I want—" She stopped, swallowing hard. Tears came to her eyes and she gestured frantically to the decorative wastebasket in the corner of the room.

Alex got it to her just in the nick of time, mentally adding "trash can" to the list of things she should replace for their host family.

BY LATE AFTERNOON, BELLE was so weak that she wasn't even asking to go the festival anymore. Her entire day had consisted of sleeping and being sick. Alex's natural maternal concern started to mutate into bleaker fear. She was having a difficult time keeping her daughter's fever down. If it went up another couple of degrees, it would hit the "seek medical attention" range. And what if Belle became dehydrated?

Medical insurance and falsified records hadn't been part of Alex's thought process when she fled Houston. She'd been ill-prepared for this. And even if Belle's fever broke and this proved to be nothing more than an inconvenient twenty-four-hour bug, the problem of records and identification wasn't going away. As Alex transferred a load of linens from the washer to the dryer, the thorny question of kindergarten in the fall once again reared its ugly head.

What in the hell am I doing?

Her nebulous, half-formed plan from the other day returned. Even if she hadn't gathered decisive ammunition against the Hargroves during her marriage, had she glimpsed and overheard enough to piece together some of their shadier activities? Perhaps if she racked her brain and started making notes, she could outline enough to make them uncomfortable, to give herself some leverage.

"Mommy?" Belle's voice was faint, but Alex had been listening for her.

"Just a sec!" She raced up the stairs. "What can I get you, baby?"

Belle scowled. "Not a baby."

"Oh, I know." Alex wrapped an arm around her daughter. "You're my big girl."

Belle cuddled closer, not saying anything for so long that Alex thought she'd fallen back asleep. When Belle finally murmured, "Big enough for ballet?" Alex knew her daughter was finally starting to feel better.

Still, it wasn't until much later that night, when Belle appeared to be in a deep sleep and hadn't been sick for several hours, that Alex felt free to take a shower. Even then, she kept it brief and left the door to the master bath open to better hear her daughter. She emerged ten minutes later, wrapped in a fluffy green towel and surrounded by steam.

Debating whether she had the energy to dry her hair or brush her teeth, she dropped across the bed. The sound of a phone ringing barely penetrated her fatigue. Since she and Belle had moved in, she periodically heard the phone or answering machine in the Comers' home office. But after a moment, Alex realized this wasn't the house phone. It was The Phone—the disposable cell Bryce had given her when he suggested that maybe she shouldn't use her real one if she wanted to stay invisible. He was the only one who had the number.

"Hello?" she answered cautiously.

"Hey, Red. How you holding up?"

"Today might not be the best day to ask," she said wryly.

The long pause on the other end made her feel guilty.

Bryce had done so much for her—she had no business whining to him.

"Sorry," she backtracked. "Belle was under the weather with a stomach bug, and I'm a little beat. Nothing's wrong."

"Um, actually…"

Dread slithered along her spine. "What is it? Your cousin coming home early? Did you see my picture up on a post office wall?"

"A private investigator came by my apartment," Bryce said.

Alex felt as if she'd plunged into icy water and was too disoriented to break the surface. *You knew this was a possibility.* Her former in-laws could afford an entire platoon of investigators if they didn't care about discretion. Still, it was alarming that anyone had tracked her to Bryce. Before crossing each other's paths at that fundraiser right before she and Chris split up, they hadn't spoken in years. They'd only been in touch a couple of times after that—it was one of the reasons she'd felt safe turning to him.

She tried to breathe normally. "D-did you talk to him?"

"For a few minutes. I got the sense he was grasping at straws. He said he was reaching out to some of your former colleagues and classmates because he represented family trying to find you. He hinted that his job was to help orchestrate a happy reunion."

Manipulative bastards. The Hargroves were exploiting her past as an orphan to generate empathy with people who'd known her.

"I played dumb," Bryce said. "Which is easier than you might think for a genius like me. Told him I couldn't recall when I'd heard from you last but that I was happy to take his number in case you got in touch. I suppose there's a remote statistical chance that he's *not* working on behalf of your evil ex-in-laws, but—"

"No, the Hargroves definitely sent him." She'd spent her entire life in the same state where she'd originally been dumped. It was ludicrous to think that her parents or other long-lost relatives just happened to be looking for her now that she was hiding from two very vindictive and powerful people. But the neighbors and friendly acquaintances she'd left behind didn't know that.

Bryce seemed to be thinking along the same lines. "You didn't tell anyone else where you were going, did you? Provide anyone with a way to reach you in case of emergency?"

"Definitely not. Chris and Belle were my only family, and you were the only friend I trusted to be entirely outside the Hargrove sphere of influence."

"And you haven't confided in anyone since you and Belle got there?"

"No, but I'm constantly afraid someone is going to catch us." A green-eyed someone with chiseled features, who lived in dangerously close proximity. She had limited practice lying, much less to a man with experience in solving crimes and observing suspects.

Before this, her only real attempt at deception had

been when she'd made quiet plans to take her daughter and leave Christopher. Even if she'd been blatant about her intentions, he would have been confident in his ability to dissuade her. It wouldn't have been the first time he'd cajoled her into staying with promises to be a better man. She'd once gotten as far as scheduling an appointment with an attorney but had canceled when she learned she was pregnant with Belle.

"Bryce, I can't thank you enough for everything you've done. You're... Thank you." The words were trite, but the gratitude she felt was too overwhelming to be captured.

He made his all-purpose *pshaw* sound. "You forget, I design games where heroes embark on quests to help others. This is the first time I've ever lived one! And it didn't even require my battling through a hell-swamp infested with zombie gators."

She laughed despite herself.

"Now that's what I like to hear," he said in a satisfied tone.

By the time they said goodbye, she was no longer in the throes of a full-blown anxiety attack. However, Bryce's call was a reminder that the Hargroves hadn't given up. If Alex had subconsciously nurtured a drop of hope that, as time healed their loss, their determination to possess their granddaughter would wane, it was gone now. *Too bad* I *can't afford a platoon of private investigators*. Even if she had more money, hiring an investigator who could be traced back to her or Bryce was risky.

No, she would have to rely on herself. It was time to start documenting that Journal of Hargrove Misdeeds. She needed to think back over eight years of marriage, every single thing she'd glimpsed or overheard, even if it had seemed innocuous at the moment. Hopefully, given enough time, she could paint a damning enough picture to protect her daughter.

BY MONDAY MORNING, BELLE'S appetite had returned with a vengeance. She was on her second helping of French toast when Alex took away the bottle of syrup her daughter seemed intent on emptying.

"Whoa! That is way too much," Alex scolded.

Belle nodded solemnly. "I deduced that from your frowny face." She'd practiced her favorite new word a lot since hearing Zane use it. "Know what else I deduce?"

"What's that?"

"Today's the day we go the festival! 'Cause you said we could if I felt better and I'm all better." To emphasize her point, she stretched *all* into three syllables.

Alex sighed inwardly. After Bryce's phone call this weekend, she was even more paranoid about being in public with her daughter. But Belle had spent a restful Sunday working on puzzles and eating soup, with no sign of nausea or fever. *I did promise.* Besides, if Alex really wanted to preserve any measure of anonymity, wasn't it best to blend in? Taking her protective stance to an extreme might make her an unintentional local mystery and draw attention to "that reclusive Hunt woman."

"All right, today's the day. If," she said, "you play

quietly in your room for a few hours so I can get some sewing done."

Belle inhaled the rest of her French toast, scurried to the sink with her dirty plate and dashed upstairs at record speed.

Well, she's definitely got her energy back. Alex tried to muster some of her own as she set up the portable sewing machine on the cleared-off kitchen table.

Last Friday, when she'd delivered one final costume to Tess, the redhead had referred her to Mrs. Turlow, an elderly lady around the corner whose arthritis had gotten too bad for her to do her own mending. Tess had mentioned what a nice job Alex did and how cheaply she was willing to work. In addition to the stitching Alex had agreed to do for Mrs. Turlow, she needed to patch some of Belle's clothes and her daughter's torn chihuahua. Belle had begun making pitiful comments about how she was not only deprived of a *real* dog, she didn't even have the comfort of her favorite stuffed puppy.

In the intermittent lulls when the sewing machine wasn't running, Alex could hear her daughter overhead, charging festival admission to princess dolls and selling them plastic fruit. Since Belle's stomach was no longer troubling her, Alex planned to finish her work just before lunchtime. They could eat at the fair once they'd dropped off Mrs. Turlow's blouses.

After a quick call to the older woman, letting her know the minor repairs were finished, it occurred to Alex that if she kept taking these seamstress odd jobs, people would need a way to contact her. Did she dare give them the number for the disposable cell phone? Even though Bryce told her it should be untraceable, the idea of sharing it made her feel nervous, exposed.

She pushed the unsettling thoughts away and called upstairs to her daughter. "Belle? Come put some shoes on so we can—"

The little girl raced down the stairs, wearing a pair of pink sparkly sneakers, carrying a floral print jacket and announcing, "Already went potty. Let's go!"

EVEN THOUGH THE CROWDS were lighter during the week than on Saturday and Sunday, there were still more than enough festivalgoers to warrant a security detail. Zane and newly promoted police sergeant Gina Sandusky were overseeing a shift of officers and volunteers. Gina had just radioed a "code seven" to let him know she was taking her lunch break. As he patrolled the area, he thought again how grateful he was to Gina for introducing her seventeen-year-old sister Beckie to Eden yesterday. The two girls had wandered the fair together on Sunday, and Beckie had agreed to pick up Eden after school today and bring her to the historic downtown area.

Was it too much to hope that Beckie's good habits would rub off on his daughter? By getting ahead with some summer courses and accelerated classes, Beckie had only needed one semester of school her senior year to earn her diploma. In August, she would leave for college and was working in the meantime to save up some money. Maybe Zane could pay Beckie to tutor his daughter if she continued to struggle in classes.

He'd praised Eden's efforts when he saw her reading a novel for class on Saturday night, but she'd dismissed him with a morose, "Not like I have anything better to do. You need friends for a social life." Hopefully, hanging out with Beckie would help in that regard, too.

Zane passed Amy Winthrop, the bartender from the Jalapeño, on the sidewalk and stopped to say hi. "Pretty day, isn't it?" After the storms at the end of last week, people had worried about bad weather dampening the festivities, but the sun had shone all weekend. If one stood in the shade, the breeze could get a little chilly, but other than that, it was a perfect spring afternoon.

She nodded. "Working outside for a few days has been a nice change from being behind the bar. Not that I don't love my bar," she added, her voice trembling. Her expression crumpled.

"Amy?" It was the first time he'd ever seen the perpetually smiling woman upset.

"Don't mind me. I'm just… You're the *last* person I should talk to right now."

"What? Why?"

"Because a smart woman wouldn't confess a premeditated crime to a lawman and I may kill Ben Torres. He's trying to talk Grace into selling the restaurant."

"But…the Jalapeño is one of the best Mexican restaurants in the entire Hill Country! And it's been in the Torres family for generations." Plus, the Jalapeño was one of the only local attractions to coax actual enthusiasm from Eden. Suddenly he wasn't too fond of Ben, either.

Glancing around at the number of people within earshot, Amy lowered her voice. "Grace doesn't publicize the fact that the Jalapeño's in trouble, but even with her attempts to revitalize the menu, we're struggling. Loans are more difficult to come by in this economy, and the restaurant needs repairs and equipment updates. She was hoping this televised cooking competition would bring in more paying customers."

"Maybe it will. The buzz all weekend has been that she's a favorite to win." Half the contestants had been eliminated so far; the remaining chefs would be appearing at the festival this week.

Amy didn't seem to hear his attempt at optimism. "I just can't believe Ben would encourage her to give up on her dreams. And that it never occurred to him that he could be putting me out of a job!"

"Any other place in the area would be lucky to have you," Zane consoled. He didn't think she was upset only about the employment issue, though. She seemed personally betrayed. Recalling how the injured officer had looked at her when Zane last had dinner with him, he wondered if Amy and Ben's relationship was less platonic than they realized.

Not that he had any intention of asking Amy about it. After his disastrous attempt last Thursday to ask Alex to dinner, he realized he was badly out of practice talking to women. Lord knew how much worse he could make things between Ben and Amy if he interfered.

"Hang in there," he offered. Lame advice, but the best he could come up with spur of the moment. He scanned the crowded Marktplatz almost desperately. If he spotted a purse-snatching in progress, he'd have a socially acceptable excuse for abruptly ending the conversation.

Amy sighed. "I shouldn't keep you. If you're here later, look for Grace. She'll be giving away yummy dessert samples at her cooking demo."

"Thanks for the heads-up."

As Amy merged back into the throng, a child's high-pitched laugh trilled out over the other ambient noise. Zane recognized the giggle even before he spotted Belle Hunt. On the playground just past the historic waterwheel, the little girl was having a high time on the swing set. She wasn't looking in his direction, but Alex, standing right behind her daughter, met Zane's gaze immediately.

Even from this distance, he could see her posture grow more rigid. He kept on his path, giving a brief wave in acknowledgment of their unspoken exchange.

Please respect my space.

Copy that.

He didn't even yield to the temptation of glancing back to see if she relaxed after it became clear he wouldn't bother her. *That is one tense woman.* Not that he blamed her. If she'd been a ward of the state, she might not have had a family until she married—and now she'd lost her husband. Zane's automatic instinct was to help in any way he could, but after the other night, she was more uncomfortable around him than ever.

He tried to tell himself that Alex was a survivor. It sounded as if her past was littered with obstacles she'd had to overcome. She and her spirited daughter would do just fine without him.

But such logical thoughts did nothing to banish the way she'd felt in his arms or his need to see her smile.

"ALEX!"

It was becoming more and more second nature to respond instantly, as if the name really was hers. She slowed, searching the crowd until she spotted Tess Fitzpatrick on the other side of the walkway. The bubbly redhead was seated at a booth with a woman who was busy painting a little boy's face.

"Look, Mommy, it's Miss Tess." Belle bolted toward the dance teacher. By the time Alex caught up, her daughter was giving Tess a detailed, mile-a-minute recap of everything they'd seen and done that afternoon.

Alex had to admit, she'd been having more fun than she'd expected. People here were incredibly welcoming. She'd felt enveloped in a sense of belonging and contentment. The only jarring moment had been when she'd been caught staring at Zane Winchester. As she'd obligingly pushed Belle on the swing, she'd noticed him crossing the sidewalk. She'd been appreciating his easy confidence and strength when he'd suddenly turned as if he could feel her gaze from a hundred yards away.

Which was ridiculous. Zane Winchester didn't have superhero senses. He was just an ordinary man. *Yeah, you keep telling yourself that.* In her years of marriage to Christopher and moving in his social circle, she'd become more jaded, deciding that qualities like integrity and generosity were extraordinary.

"Alex?" Tess snapped her fingers. "You okay? You looked like maybe you've been out in the sun too long."

Alex shook her head. "I'm just brain-dead from trying to keep up with Belle."

Tess grinned. "I know the feeling. By the end of an hour with half a dozen tap-dancing preschoolers, I'm always toast."

Belle tugged on the bottom of Alex's short-sleeved sweater. "Can I get my face painted?"

"It's free," Tess said. "The only catch is, we're amateur volunteers."

"What's *am-a-teur?*" Belle drew the word out slowly.

"It means I'm not very good," Tess admitted. "But as I tell my students, we get better at everything with practice. Have a seat."

Belle scrambled into the folding chair.

"How about a heart or a smiling sun?" Tess suggested. "Or I could do a rainbow."

"Can you paint a chihuahua?" Belle asked.

"Um…probably not. But for you, I'm willing to try." She dipped a brush in some brown paint and went to work.

"That tickles!"

"Sorry." As Tess waited for the girl to quit wiggling, she asked Alex, "So where are you two headed next?"

"I promised Belle we'd split a funnel cake, but after that we should go home."

"Oh." Tess looked disappointed. "My shift is over in about ten minutes, and I'm meeting up with Lorelei Keller. We're going to stop by the celebrity chef demonstrations. I thought maybe you'd like to join us for the free dessert tasting."

"Dessert?" Belle bounced in her chair, jostling Tess's brush.

The dance teacher winced. "If you're not still, this chihuahua's gonna end up looking like abstract art."

Belle did her best statue impression until Tess was done. Then she whipped her head around. "Mommy, can we stay for the dessert? Please!"

"You're getting funnel cake, remember? And then home for a bath. You smell like that pony you were riding."

Since it had been a slow afternoon and Belle had been enjoying herself so much, Sam, the cowboy in charge of the pony ring, had given Belle extra time before a line began forming.

Tess changed the subject by holding out a mirror. "Want to see how it turned out?"

Belle studied her reflection. "It looks like a chocolate chip cookie. That's okay, Miss Tess. I like cookies."

The redhead laughed. "Glad you approve. Now you go with your mom without fussing, or she'll think I'm a bad influence on you. You guys enjoy your funnel cake."

"Thanks," Alex said. "Oh, and thanks again for recommending me to Mrs. Turlow. The extra cash helps keep us in sidewalk chalk and cookie dough."

"How much extra are you looking to make?" Tess

asked. Her cheeks flushed. "Is it rude to ask about your finances? I only meant, I can pass around your name and number. Between growing up here and running the studio, I know just about everyone."

Alex's stomach tightened in a nervous spasm. The idea of Tess giving everyone in a fifty-mile radius her name and contact information made her want to throw up. She swallowed. "That's sweet, Tess. I'll think about it. But one of the advantages of this house-sitting gig instead of a traditional job is getting to spend this extra one-on-one time with Belle before she starts school. I don't want to cut into that too much."

"Understood. You have my number if you change your mind. Heck, call me just if you want to go out for a girls' night sometime! There's a place that does weekly trivia. Or, I'm not entirely inept at pool."

"*I* am. But I really appreciate the offer. You've been wonderful about making me feel like I fit in." It was a feeling that had eluded Alex most of her life. When she was a kid, she'd stuck out among her classmates because she didn't have a real family. Later, even when she'd considered herself unbelievably lucky to be with Chris, she'd felt out of her depth with his rich friends. And when the couples they knew had started having kids and she couldn't… "Everyone we've met here has been so neighborly."

"Mister Zane's our neighbor," Belle chimed, always wanting to be part of the conversation.

"Oh, that's right. Zane Winchester," Tess said in a dreamy tone. She fanned herself with her hand. It was clear *she* wouldn't have any misgivings about living in close proximity to him. "If y'all ever have a subdivision barbecue, would you pretty please invite me as your guest?"

"Done," Alex promised.

"Or," Tess amended with a gleam in her eye, "we could be proactive. Why wait? You can have a backyard cookout. A small, intimate affair including myself and the good Ranger."

"What do you need me for?" Alex asked. "Just ask him to dinner sometime. I wouldn't want to be a third wheel."

"Oh, I don't actually see myself with a stoic lawman raising a teenage daughter. He's just really fun to look at. Don't you think so?" she prompted when Alex didn't respond.

"I guess." It was probably a more enjoyable experience for women who could be around him without worrying he might discover their secret identities and have them hauled off to jail.

Belle sighed theatrically. "I sure am hungry!" she said to no one in particular.

"That's my cue to leave," Alex said in a stage whisper. Normally, she would have reprimanded her daughter for the rude interjection. At the moment, though, she was too grateful for the excuse to stop discussing Zane.

"Now I'm *really* hungry," Belle whined. "And my feet hurt."

"Then it's good that we're going home, so you can

rest your feet," Alex reasoned. "The booth is right over there." *And they'd darn well better have funnel cake.*

Unfortunately, Alex hadn't realized that the last vendor was sold out of funnel cakes until after she and Belle had waited in line. As sunset approached, more townspeople were arriving to have dinner and enjoy the bands scheduled to play that night. Alex and Belle had only stood in line ten minutes, but that was like an hour in four-year-old time. The cashier had tried to interest the girl in a caramel-dipped apple, and, when that failed, she'd pointed out the nearest booth that also sold funnel cakes.

Alex tried to be patient with her increasingly cranky child. She knew the little girl was tired. They both were. *Last stop, and then we're done for the evening.*

Staring at the people ahead of them, Belle whimpered. "Do I hafta wait in this line, too?"

"You do if you want funnel cake," Alex said firmly. "Or we could just skip it and go home. Your choice."

"Cake," Belle said. She stopped complaining, but after a couple of minutes passed, she plopped down on the ground.

Alex didn't say anything until Belle began tunneling her fingers into the dirt, sifting it through her hands and letting the breeze catch it. "Stop that. You can't share my funnel cake with filthy hands. Wouldn't you rather stand up than get your clothes all dirty?"

"No," Belle said mulishly.

Alex was contemplating lifting her child bodily and carrying her to the car when she noticed the bench to the right of the concessions window. "How about you go sit over there?" The seat was currently unoccupied and since the line would keep moving toward the bench, Belle would always be in her line of vision. "Want to do that?"

Belle nodded happily, skipping toward the seat with temporarily renewed energy.

All at once, the line didn't seem so much a chore as a respite. Alex exhaled deeply, enjoying the moment of peace and quiet before the ride back to the house. Unless Belle fell asleep in her car seat, she'd probably keep up a steady monologue of her opinions about the festival.

Finally Alex made her way to the counter. "One funnel cake, please."

"With just the powdered sugar, or do you want the deluxe version?" the teenage boy asked. "That includes chocolate syrup, whipped cream and a cherry on top."

Because there just wasn't enough fat and sugar in the regular version? "Oh, all right. We'll splurge and take the works." *S*he didn't see how it could be any worse for a person than the deep fried cheesecake slices she'd seen for sale earlier in the day.

"Coming right up," he said.

She peered around the corner of the booth to give Belle a triumphant thumbs-up. Then she handed the cashier a twenty-dollar bill and reached for a stack of napkins while she waited for her change.

"Oh, crap." He glared at the cash register.

"Problem?" Alex asked.

"I shut the drawer without thinking. Sorry. That automatically ends the transaction. I need my supervisor to open it and authorize your change."

Alex forced herself to be magnanimous. "No problem." She'd once worked a hellish three months at a fast-food drive-through window. Mistakes happened. At least they were getting their funnel cake.

Besides, judging from the malevolent look the supervisor gave the kid, he was going to get an earful later. No need for Alex to contribute to his lousy afternoon.

Once the problem had been settled, she thanked the guy and his manager and whirled, eager to go. But she collided with the man who'd been stepping up to place his order. Alex managed to hold on to her funnel cake but dropped the napkins and forks she'd been holding.

"I apologize," she told the man. "I wasn't watching because I was in a hurry to get to my daughter." She gestured toward the bench, and her blood froze.

Belle was gone.

Chapter Six

Oh my God, they've got her. Gone was the cozy sense of community Alex had enjoyed earlier in the day. As she raced away from the concessions counter and past the bench, the falling dusk and bustling crowd seemed like threats to Belle's safety. The booths and vendor tables created a hateful labyrinth, slowing Alex's progress and limiting her field of vision.

"Belle!" She darted around a platform where people were invited to "step right up" and play midway-style games. "*Belle!*" Not seeing any sign of her daughter in one direction, Alex backtracked and tried another. "Josie?" Panic trumped cautionary protocol.

She tried to tell herself that she hadn't looked away from her daughter for long. How far could the girl have realistically gone? But that answer depended on whether she was being carried. No, no, no. It wasn't fully dark yet, and they were surrounded by people. Wouldn't someone have noticed an uncooperative girl being abducted?

A hundred scenarios played through her head, each worse than the last, and Alex knew she needed to enlist help. Zane and other law officials had been present all day. She just had to find one. She pushed her way to the front of a line and frantically explained the situation, asking for directions to the nearest emergency checkpoint.

"Is there like a first aid station—or, or—" She broke off, abruptly realizing that she'd started crying and couldn't choke out any more words.

An older woman with a kindly face and wire-rim glasses patted her on the shoulder. "Just try to breathe, dear. Name's Ava. And you are...?"

"Hea— Alexandra Hunt. Alex. My daughter's Belle. She's o-only four. I don't know how she got away from me so quickly. Sh-she—"

Ava pointed at the man working the register. "Why don't you give Paul here your phone number so he can call if she wonders back this way? Meanwhile, you and I will go give Belle's description to an officer."

Though her hands were shaking almost too hard to hold a pen, Alex managed to write her cell number for Paul. As the two women navigated the crowd, Ava talked nonstop, her voice soothing.

"Many years ago, I misplaced my niece Emily at the San Antonio River Walk. Longest ten minutes of my life. I know just how you feel, dear, but I'm sure your Belle is fine. Ah, here we are."

They reached a trailer that had a Fredericksburg PD sign on the door, obviously a makeshift HQ for officers working at the festival. A tall blonde with a strong jawline introduced herself as Sergeant Sandusky and immediately asked for Belle's description. Alex pulled out the photo she kept on her key ring, a snapshot of Belle laughing at the camera. *Please, Lord, don't let her be hurt.* Alex detailed the clothes her daughter had been wearing, ending with, "And she got her face painted. There's a picture on her cheek that looks sort of like a mutant chocolate-chip cookie."

"Give me just a moment to radio out this description to everyone," the blonde said, walking away from where Alex sat.

Ava leaned forward to squeeze her hand reassuringly. "Can I get you a cup of water, dear?"

"Yes. Thank you." Alex couldn't care less about getting something to drink, but she needed to call Bryce. If he could give her a description of the P.I. who'd come looking for her, then she was giving it to the police. She had to, if it would help them locate her baby.

But Bryce's phone went straight to voice mail. Fresh tears burned her eyes as she thought about the precious seconds she might be losing. Should she tell them about the possible lead even if she didn't have any concrete information? Would it help the police at all, or only ensure that she and Belle were ultimately separated?

I don't know what to do. She lifted her gaze to the ceiling in beseeching, unarticulated prayer. All she'd wanted was to protect her child, to be a good mother. But she'd failed.

WHEN ZANE GOT THE MISSING child alert, he'd been on his way back to the trailer to wait for his evening replacement. He'd given Eden some cash to buy them pulled pork barbecue to take home for dinner. As soon as Gina said the child's name was Belle Hunt, he broke into a run. He cleared the first two steps without even touching them, his eyes going straight to the hunched figure in the chair.

"Alex!"

Her face was deathly pale, her eyes wild. But they lit with something like relief when she saw him. "Zane, oh, God, I lost her. Help me find her. Please."

"Of course." He crossed the small interior. "Sergeant Sandusky, this is my neighbor Alex Hunt. I'm well acquainted with her daughter. I was about to round up Eden and call it a day. Can Eden stay here while Alex and I canvass the festival grounds? Do you have a current photo of her?"

"I've already scanned it," Gina reported.

"Good." He helped Alex to her feet. "Take me back to where you last saw her, and we'll go from there."

She nodded, looking slightly calmer. "I was getting her funnel cake. She really wanted funnel cake. She was mad we couldn't stay for the dessert sampling, but not mad enough to run off on her own!"

Zane slid his arm around her and escorted her down the trailer stairs. He'd worked a lot of cases in his career and knew to remain analytical, never emotional. Still, it was difficult not to recall how Eden had looked as a four-year-old with pigtails and overalls, difficult not to imagine the hell he'd be suffering if this had happened to her.

"It's going to be okay," he said. "Belle's a tough cookie. She's probably a lot less scared than you are. But you know what? I think deep down you're pretty tough, too."

"No, I'm a mess. I…I can't lose her, Zane. She's my entire world."

They were close to the place where she said she'd bought the funnel cakes when he spotted Grace Torres walking with a man who also wore a chef's jacket. "Grace!"

He hurried his pace, trotting after her. "Grace, I understand you had a dessert demo a little while ago?"

She nodded, flicking a puzzled glance toward Alex's tearstained face. "Just finished up."

"And you gave samples to the crowd?" Zane asked. If someone walking past Belle had mentioned they were headed for the dessert tasting and the little girl had thought it was close by, was she bold enough to have followed? He held out the picture Alex had given him. "This is Belle Hunt. Any chance you saw her? She has a sweet tooth, so I thought she might have gravitated toward a free dessert."

Grace's pretty features filled with sympathy, and she concentrated hard on the photo, obviously hoping to recognize the kid. "No, I'm sorry." She turned to the other chef with her, her tone hopeful. "Ty? Did you notice her?"

He shook his head, looking equally apologetic not to have more useful information. "Anything we can do to help with the search?"

"We already have police and over a dozen festival volunteers looking," Zane said. "We'll find her." For Alex's sake, he put as much conviction as he could in his voice, rubbing her shoulder as he spoke. The way she sagged against him spoke volumes about how scared she was.

"Can I at least help check the women's restrooms?" Grace offered. "Maybe she just had to go potty and got lost."

"That would—" A burst of static from his radio interrupted. *Let it be good news.* "Winchester here."

"This is Sandusky. We've got her, sir. Safe and sound."

Alex was eerily quiet as tears poured down her face. Her body shook so hard it probably registered on the Richter scale. Even though the ordeal was over, Zane's heart twisted. After everything else she'd been through, he couldn't imagine how she'd survive anything happening to Belle.

"Sandusky, put the little girl on so she can say hello," Zane instructed. "There's someone here who needs to hear her voice."

There was another crackle of static, then, "Mommy?"

Alex reached out blindly, squeezing Zane's hand. "Punkin, are you all right? What happened? Where were you? You were supposed to stay on that bench!"

"I wanted to ask a woman if I could pet her cute little dog, but I couldn't catch up. And then I couldn't find you," Belle said miserably.

"Oh, baby, I'm so glad you're okay. And I love you more than anything! But you are in *so much* trouble."

"Yeah." Belle sniffled piteously. "I already deduced that."

ALEX'S ONLY CLEAR THOUGHT was to get back to her daughter's side. Immediately. She zigzagged through the dinner crowd and the maze of booths. She restrained herself from outright running, but acknowledged on some level that she was walking too fast. When she veered off the sidewalk to cut around some people, her foot struck a hole. Her ankle twisted to the side and she might have gone down if Zane hadn't been there. He gently caught her arm, angling her so that she fell into his side rather than onto the ground. He absorbed her weight effortlessly.

"Steady there," he murmured. "I understand your hurry, but why don't we slow down?" He gestured to a building behind her. "You might even want to go splash some cold water on your face."

Rather than scare her child with bright red eyes and puffy features? "I look awful, don't I?"

Instead of instantly confirming her suspicions or dismissing them with a kind lie, he paused to really examine her. He brushed strands of disheveled hair out of her eyes and met her gaze tenderly. "You look like a mom who loves her kid. Belle's lucky to have you. And you must be a nicer parent than me, because you know what I'd be doing in your shoes? Dawdling. Giving her time to Consider the Consequences of Her Actions."

He punctuated the words with finger quotes, making it sound like the title of some child-rearing brochure.

"I had a foster mother who used to do that. Maggie Reardon," she recalled. The Reardons had been good parents and had taught her a lot during her stay with them. "Whenever we screwed up, she'd send us to sit on our beds and wait for sentencing. The punishments we got were never as bad as the time we spent sweating it out beforehand."

Zane grinned. "Exactly."

Alex cast a glance over her shoulder at the restroom. "I suppose I could take a quick second."

He nodded approvingly. "Belle's with Eden and Gina. She'll be absolutely fine until you get there. You have my word on that."

She hadn't realized until he suggested it how much she needed a moment to herself. All the adrenaline that had been dumped into her system had left her shaky and nauseous. What little eye makeup she'd put on before the festival had become inky tracks across her tear-blotched face. Her hair was standing on end, and her nose was running. A blush heated her cheeks. Zane had seen her like this? Yikes. Good thing she hadn't wanted to date him because, with *this* memory fresh in his mind, it was a good bet he'd never ask her out again.

But even though she couldn't get involved with him romantically, she regretted that she'd been so quick to reject his previous overtures of friendship. Because today, she'd been damn glad to have him as a friend. When he'd told her back at the police trailer that everything would be okay, she'd actually believed him. Zane would make everything right. He was a man of his word who would do whatever it took to get her daughter safely back in her arms. She'd trusted him, this man she'd only known for a couple of weeks, more than she'd trusted her own husband by the end of their marriage. Zane was steady and honest. Guilt twisted inside her and Alex closed her eyes, reminding herself that she wasn't deceiving people by choice.

What was that saying? *Necessity is the mother of invention.*

She faced her reflection again. "Doesn't mean I have to like it." She couldn't tell Zane who she was and she couldn't begin to repay him for his assistance today. But he'd asked her for a favor the other night. At the very least, she could accommodate his request about Eden.

When she met him back outside, he handed her a cup of coffee. "Decaf," he said. "Figured your nerves were keyed up enough already."

"Thank you." She took the packets of sugar and creamer he handed her, touched anew by his simple acts of kindness. Chris had tended toward showy flamboyant gestures meant to impress; basic consideration had often eluded him. "I owe you. And not just for the coffee. I'm so glad you were here."

He touched the brim of his white hat. "Just doin' my job, ma'am."

As they walked, words tumbled out of her. She knew she was babbling, but Zane let her, listening without interruption. "The second I realized she wasn't on that bench, I… It was like my mind splintered. But when you walked into the trailer, I could think again. It was still horrible, not knowing where she was, but I didn't feel like I was careening out of control anymore." Even though they hadn't been the ones to find her, she'd felt better going back to the scene and actively searching than she had cramped in that trailer, left with nothing to do but envision worst-case scenarios. "Zane, about Eden babysitting sometime? Absolutely. I can hire her for—"

"Whoa." He drew up short on the sidewalk, frowning at her. "Alex, you had valid points for not being comfortable with her watching Belle. If anything, you're going to be even more nervous about leaving your daughter after tonight. Like I said, I was doing my job, but even if I were a plumber, I would've helped. There was a little girl's safety at stake! You're not indebted to me simply because I behaved with normal human decency."

She flinched. "I wasn't trying to insult you. I just wanted…needed…to feel like I could give you something in return."

He stared at her with those piercing eyes, his jaw set.

"Let me find a way to say thank you," she pleaded. "To help get rid of this godawful powerless feeling. You have a favorite dessert? I bake."

"German chocolate cake."

"Then you can expect one tomorrow."

They were in front of the trailer when he said, "How about this? You and Belle come over for dinner, and we'll have the cake for dessert."

She rolled her eyes in exasperation. "Zane. I'm supposed to be repaying you, not making you cook for us."

"You and Eden can do the dishes—give her a chance to confide in a woman. She's been too angry to admit it, but she must miss her mama. It'll be good for her."

Dinner with the Winchesters? "All right," Alex agreed quickly, before she could talk herself out of it. "Tomorrow night it is."

"Poor Belle." Eden steered the grocery cart up the canned fruits and vegetables aisle Tuesday afternoon. "She looked so terrified when they brought her into the trailer last night."

"I'm sure she was. Of course, the whole thing could have been avoided if she'd stayed where her mother told her to wait instead of wandering away. You know, parents have *reasons* for the rules they enforce," Zane said pointedly. "Children should listen more and argue less."

"You are not a subtle man," Eden observed.

"I have other admirable qualities," he informed her as he reached for some green beans.

"Dad!" His daughter sounded scandalized. "You aren't planning on serving those to the Hunts." She didn't even make it a question.

"Is there some problem with green beans I don't know about?" They were his standard accompaniment to grilled steaks and baked potatoes.

She removed the can from his hand gingerly, as if taking a sharp object away from a hapless toddler. "Get fresh produce. We'll snap them and roast them with some olive oil and a touch of vinegar. If *I* were going out with a guy, I'd want him to make some effort, not just open a can."

His brain tried to go in two directions at once—wondering if Eden had mistaken tonight for a romantic dinner and the fatherly certainty that she was too young to "go out" with anyone. He didn't get a chance to comment on either circumstance before she continued.

"You do want to make a good impression on her, right? This is your chance to start fresh. Because Alex did not like you before." His daughter made the statement with lots of conviction.

And she says I'm *not subtle?* "I don't think Alex disliked me personally. She lost her husband, and people put up walls after they get hurt. It's a means of protecting themselves."

Eden rounded the corner, not meeting his eyes as she asked, "Is that what happened with you? After the divorce? Mom's hooked up with tons of guys, but you're still alone. Is that because you have a wall?"

He tamped down sarcastic thoughts about the type of role model Val was and pondered Eden's question. "I date," he defended himself. "Occasionally. It's just not my top priority. My work—" At the hurt that flashed across her face, he stopped himself.

His daughter should have been his priority. Alex proclaimed herself to be an overprotective mother—and maybe she was—but no one could question her devotion to Belle.

He scrubbed a hand over his face. "Eden, I—"

"Are you getting a bottle of wine?" she asked. "And what about candles?"

"There's going to be a four-year-old at the table," he reminded her. "I'm not sure alcohol and fire hazards are entirely appropriate. Look, Eden, about—"

"Oh, my favorite potato chips are on sale!" She abandoned the cart and stalked past him, not letting him finish.

Speaking of those protective walls...

He was frustrated by his inability to get through to her but reminded himself to be patient. It was a skill he'd honed on the job. He thought of the cold cases he'd helped solve, of the months of legwork and diligence that had gone into them. Another thing he'd learned from a career where various agencies cooperated to bring down the bad guys was to know when to call in reinforcements. He truly believed that Alex might be able to relate to his daughter in ways he couldn't yet.

The opportunity to spend more time with his beautiful neighbor was simply a bonus.

ALL DAY LONG, BELLE had been subdued, as if trying to make up for her mistake yesterday with an appropriately somber attitude. But as the hour grew closer to dinnertime and their visit to the Winchesters, she couldn't contain herself any longer.

"Eden will be there, right? She likes me. And Dolly likes me, too. Do you think I'll get to play with her?"

"I think that if you *ever* want me to consider getting you a dog, you'd better not chase after another one again," Alex said matter-of-factly. She finished rinsing the dishes she'd used to bake the double layer German chocolate cake and glanced down. "What are you wearing?"

"Tonight is special," Belle said, as if that explained wearing her black velvet Christmas dress over a pair of sweatpants…or the iridescent fairy wings strapped to her shoulders.

Alex pinched the bridge of her nose. "You don't have to wear such a fancy dress." Although, as fast as Belle was growing, clothes from last December wouldn't fit her much longer. "Or you could keep the dress on and lose the pants."

"But my legs were cold," Belle explained patiently.

Fine, but were the wings really necessary? Then again, it wasn't as if the Winchesters weren't acquainted with Belle's unique fashion statements. And Alex was running late in getting herself ready. She should be changing into a shirt that wasn't smeared with batter, not standing around discussing sartorial choices with her kid.

"I'll be right back," she said. "Why don't you put your shoes on?"

"Yes, ma'am," Belle agreed promptly, her impression of a perfectly behaved child. She'd been making such a concerted effort today that it would have been amusing—except that Alex's bonedeep terror was still too fresh in her mind.

Alex wished she possessed her daughter's self-assurance when it came to selecting clothes. Instead, she second-guessed herself as she zipped up a black skirt. When was the last time she'd even worn a skirt? In her former life, depending on the events of her social calendar, she might wear two designer gowns in the same week. But now she lived a decidedly more casual existence. Suddenly, a skirt with a fitted rust-colored sweater seemed like she was trying too hard. She had a mad urge to rifle through Belle's closet. It must be liberating to strap on a glittery pair of nylon wings and call it a day.

"Oh, this is ridiculous," she muttered to her reflection. "Women all over the world like to look good—it's how cosmetics companies stay in business." Her dangling earrings and the copper eye shadow she applied had nothing to do with Zane Winchester.

Hoping the temperature wouldn't drop too low tonight, she stepped into a pair of black sandals and left her room. "Belle? You ready?"

This got another "yes, ma'am."

Alex went into the kitchen for the cake, stopping momentarily when she caught sight of her daughter's rubber rain boots. "Are you sure those are what you want to wear?"

Belle nodded. "I wanna show Eden the ducks."

Why the heck not—if it got cold this evening, Belle's feet would probably stay warmer than her own.

It was already dark outside, but Zane had turned on a number of lights for them, including the bulb over his front porch and the spotlight on the side of his house. In his backyard, little white lights twinkled above the fence. She could already smell something yummy on the grill. Eden must have been watching for them because she opened the door just as Alex raised her fist to knock.

"Hi!" the teenager chirped. "We're so glad you could make it. Ms. Hunt, you look *really* nice."

"Thank you."

"What about me?" Belle demanded. "Like my wings?"

"They're the best," Eden answered without a trace of condescension. "Dad's out on the deck. Belle and I can hang out in my room while you adults talk. I've got some of my old favorite animated movies on DVD."

"She likes movies, but I'm not sure you'll be able to pry her away from the dog."

Dolly had come bounding to the front door, and Belle had plopped down to hug her hello. The dog was licking her face in greeting. Between fits of giggles, Belle shrieked in mock-protest.

Alex followed her young hostess through the house. This home was smaller than the one she and Belle were staying in, cozier. The color coordination was less forced, as well. Kelsey and Dave's house was full of a lot of cranberry, accented with lighter mauves; then there was the master bathroom in graduating shades of sea-foam that probably had names like "misty morning mint." At Zane's, there wasn't so much a color scheme as a lot of sanded and stained wood paired with comfortable-looking furniture. Not fancy, but warm and welcoming.

Like the man who lived here.

When Alex paused to set the cake on the kitchen counter, Eden threw open the back door.

"They're here!" She lowered her voice to an aggrieved whisper. "If you'd bought wine like I'd suggested, this would be a good time to offer her a glass. It makes you look sophisticated."

Zane humored his daughter by hanging his head, seemingly abashed. But as soon as the teenager had walked away, he grinned at Alex. "I have a 2012 lemon-lime soda I've been saving for a special occasion. We could open that, let it breathe."

"Lemon-lime? No, no, no." She indicated the plate of marinated filets next to him. "You should have red with steak. Maybe a robust fruit punch?"

"I should've known that." He slapped his forehead. "Shoot, Eden's right. I am hopelessly unsophisticated."

Alex chuckled. "You're talking to a woman whose social life is largely comprised of tea parties with teddy bears. Not that I'm complaining," she clarified. "Sometimes I think sophistication is just an excuse to be pretentious. I'll take backyard steaks and punch over snobby formal dinners with well-dressed hypocrites any day."

He leaned against the deck, his eyebrows raised. "Sound like you're speaking from experience. Know a lot of well-dressed hypocrites?"

"What?" She blinked, reminding herself that Zane didn't miss much. She had to be careful about even small comments regarding her previous lifestyle. "A lot? Nah. But even one's too many. Mmm." She drew in a deep breath, grateful for an easy excuse to change the subject. "Sure smells good. I noticed that even from the Comers' yard."

"Chili-lime shrimp appetizers." He removed the skewers from the grill. "Figured we could snack on those while I'm cooking the main course. The potatoes and green beans are already in the oven. *Fresh* green beans," he added. "My daughter was insistent. All kidding aside, can I get you a drink? Soda, sweet tea, a beer?"

"A glass of iced tea would be great, thanks." She followed him back inside, examining her surroundings. "I really like your place. It's not exactly what I would have expected, but… " She trailed off, realizing she sounded incongruously surprised for someone who'd already been here. "The first time I was over, I guess I wasn't really paying attention."

He set two glasses on the counter with a knowing smile. "Too intent on grabbing the pasta and getting the hell out of Dodge?"

She groaned. "I've been a lousy neighbor, haven't I?"

"Well…we probably won't be electing you onto the homeowner's association board anytime soon," he conceded. "But I've lived next to less desirable people. When I was in college, my neighbor was a guy with a drinking problem who kept locking himself out of his apartment and banging on my door at three in the morning."

"Wish one of my college neighbors *had* locked herself out more," Alex grumbled, recalling some sleepless nights—including one immediately preceding a major exam. "Unfortunately, she kept coming home. With her boyfriend. They were not a quiet couple."

Zane laughed. "I gather you don't mean they watched the television with the volume up too loud?"

"Um." Her cheeks warmed, and she resisted the urge to press the cold glass of tea against her skin. "No."

As they returned to the deck, Zane asked curiously, "What is it about my house that defied your expectations?"

"Just that it's so individual. I used to live in a neighborhood where all the homes looked like they'd been churned out on an assembly line. I swear I used to park in the wrong driveway some nights because I couldn't tell them apart. Your house is nothing like Kelsey's."

"This is an older neighborhood, constructed before builders began making everything so uniform. A little nonconformity can be refreshing."

She sipped her tea. "Glad you feel that way. You should see what my daughter's wearing."

"I like what *you're* wearing." He cut his gaze toward her, then back to the grill. "You look great."

"Thank you." The stab of pleasure she felt at his words forced her to admit the truth. No matter how foolish it was—and not that she would *ever* act on it—she was attracted to Zane. And she had enough feminine pride that she'd wanted to be attractive for him, too.

"So." He kept his attention on the steaks. "How do you know Kelsey?"

Damn. Conversational land mines like that one

were exactly why she'd wanted to keep her distance from Zane in the first place. But after what he'd done for her at the festival… She couldn't ignore someone who'd helped her in a crisis. Besides, trying to pretend he didn't live right next door wouldn't change reality. Spending the next five months trying to pretend she wasn't home and averting her eyes whenever they crossed paths in town would be ridiculously suspicious behavior. She just had to figure out the best strategy for times like these, when he asked her direct questions. Hadn't she heard once that the most effective lies were partial truths?

"I, uh, don't know her. We've never actually met in person, but we have a mutual acquaintance." She jabbed her index finger toward the plate of shrimp. "Is it too soon to try one of those? I'm starving."

"Help yourself, please. That's what they're for. How do you and Belle like your steaks?" he asked. "My default mode for cooking them is medium rare, but Eden's been reminding me since she moved in that not everyone enjoys a red center."

That led to a discussion of food and swapped stories about how they'd coaxed their respective daughters into trying new dishes and eating vegetables. The anecdotes were entertaining, but ultimately superficial, the kind of thing she could have told total strangers in a pediatrician's waiting room. Harmless small talk.

So why couldn't she shake the feeling that, with every passing second, a bond was forming, that she was perilously close to crossing an invisible line?

Chapter Seven

It was one of the best meals Alex had experienced since coming to the Hill Country, thanks as much to the company as the perfectly grilled steak. And she wasn't the only one who'd had a good time tonight. Belle was in her element—giggling with Eden, showing off for Zane by reciting nature facts and spelling words out loud.

"But can you spell *dessert?*" Zane challenged, his green eyes twinkling. "Because I think it's time for cake."

"Cake!" Belle agreed.

Eden moaned in protest. "No offense, Ms. Hunt, it looks delicious, but I'm stuffed."

"I'm with you," Alex said, too full to contemplate any more food.

"How about this?" Zane proposed. "Belle and I can take Dolly for a walk around the neighborhood. Maybe we'll all feel like cake afterward. Does that sound okay with you?" he asked Alex.

"Sounds perfect." She knew he wanted to give Eden the chance to open up to her. And if there was one thing Belle got even more excited about than dessert, it was dogs. "But you had better stay right next to Mr. Zane, young lady!"

"Yes, ma'am." Belle was the picture of wide-eyed innocence. "I'll be an angel."

Zane leaned across the table toward Alex, lowering his voice to a teasing whisper. "She does have the wings for it."

He whistled for the dog and instructed Eden to clear the dishes.

"I'll help," Alex volunteered. She rose from her chair, grinning at the picture the departing trio made as they left the house—the tall Texas Ranger, the tail-wagging mutt and the four-year-old in her bright blue boots with yellow ducks. Eden watched, too, looking less charmed.

"Everything all right?" Alex asked cautiously. "If we're cutting in on your time with your dad, we—"

"It's not that. I'm glad you guys moved in next door." She carried a couple of plates to the sink. "But I think Dad wishes I were Belle's age. He might like me better if I still wore tiaras and fairy wings." Her voice was a heartrending blend of bitterness and vulnerability.

"Your dad loves you. I can tell you that with absolute one hundred percent certainty."

"That's not the same as liking me. He *has* to love me. It's a parental obligation."

Alex didn't comment on her own experience with that particular obligation.

"But he doesn't get me," Eden said. "He treats me like a kid most of the time. I don't think he wants me to grow up."

"Try to cut him some slack," Alex advised. "It's hard for us to watch our babies get older. I'm freaking out just at the thought of Belle going to kindergarten—the stuff you're facing in high school is far more daunting to a parent."

Eden made a noncommittal sound and began filling the sink with liquid dish soap and hot water.

Alex gathered the rest of the dishes. "If you don't mind my being nosy, how is school going?"

"Classes are okay, I guess. I was behind on some of my work, but I'm catching up," she said defensively.

"Good for you. It's never easy to change schools mid-year."

"Thank you!" Eden tossed up her hands, splattering suds across the counter. "Dad totally doesn't understand. He lived here his whole life, except for the few years when he went away to college. He has no concept of what it's like to be the new kid!"

"He may not have firsthand experience with it, but I'll bet he'd be willing to listen if you wanted to have a conversation about it."

Eden didn't respond. Her skeptical look spoke for itself.

"Or, if you really need to talk to someone who's been through it," Alex heard herself offer, "I'm available. I was the new kid in plenty of schools and different homes. Foster homes," she elaborated.

"For real? So you, like, didn't have parents?"

"I had some great foster parents over the years." She chose not to dwell on the less than greats. "One of them explained to me that I was having trouble making friends because I seemed too angry. I didn't understand what she meant at first. It's not as if I was starting fights or screaming at people. I never argued with my teachers or foster siblings. But I also never smiled at anyone, never opened myself to the opportunity of making friends."

Eden cocked her head. "You're saying you had a wall. To protect yourself."

"Something along those lines, yeah."

"Huh." Eden picked up the scrub brush, muttering, "Guess he understands some stuff, after all."

They fell into a rhythm of washing and drying the dishes together. A few minutes passed before the teenager asked, "Are you saying that if I smile at school and let down my wall or whatever, I'll get friends?"

"I think it's worth trying."

"What about you?" Eden looked her square in the eye. "Are you trying to make new friends?"

I wasn't. But it seemed to be happening anyway. "I'm friends with Tess Fitzpatrick," she said slowly. "And, uh, your father. And you? I'd like it if we could be friends."

Apparently, that was the right answer. A smile lit the teen's face, and she raised a wet soapy hand. "Deal."

They sealed their newfound friendship with a squishy handshake that made Alex laugh; she ignored the warning voice inside that cautioned she couldn't build friendships with people she was deceiving.

"IF I'D KNOWN THE CAKE was that good, I would have skipped dinner and gone straight for the German chocolate," Zane said.

The girls had scarfed down their pieces and retreated to Eden's room, leaving the adults to savor their dessert at a more leisurely pace.

"Glad you enjoyed it," Alex told him. "But I'm kicking myself for not remembering to buy vanilla ice cream to go with it. That makes it perfect."

"This was already pretty close to perfect," he countered. The look in his eye made her wonder if he was talking about the cake or their evening together.

She hadn't dated since college, since before Chris. But back in her dating days, she would have considered this night perfect. The only thing missing was the kiss at the end. Her gaze slid to Zane's mouth. She'd only kissed one person for the last decade. What would it be like to—

Alex shot out of her chair, appalled at the direction her thoughts had taken. "Well, thanks again for having us!" Her voice was too high. What she'd meant as cheerful had come out shrill.

He stood, too, looking perplexed. "Is that goodbye?"

"It is a school night."

"Only for Eden." He laughed. "And eight-thirty hasn't been her bedtime in years."

"Right. Of course. But it's Belle's bedtime."

"One cup of coffee before you go?" Zane asked, going to the counter. He poured water into the coffeemaker. "I haven't had a chance to interrogate you yet about your time alone with my daughter. Did she sound like she might grow to be content here, or like she was squirreling away money to hop a westbound bus?"

"I don't think she's making plans to run off in the night," Alex assured him. "She's struggling with being an outsider, though. I let her know I was available if she needs to vent. I've been the new kid."

"And the new adult," he teased lightly. "How are you settling in? Glad you came to Fredericksburg?"

Tonight she was. "Yeah. But our being here is only temporary. Eventually the Comers are gonna want their house back." She tried to make it a joke, but her voice was tinged with sadness. What in the hell was she going to do when they had to leave? Belle had been a trouper, but she was already growing attached to the people she'd met.

"Where is it that you and Belle are from?" he asked.

"Austin. Th-the Barton Creek area." She and Bryce had discussed her "address" before she'd been given her new driver's license. It was simplest to pick a place in Texas—one that wouldn't be such an automatic link to her Houston in-laws or her partner in crime in Dallas— and she was familiar with Austin from her college days. Although, considering how much had undoubtedly changed since then, if anyone began discussing specifics, she would have to demur that her past was still too raw and that she preferred not to think about it. The real problem was what her daughter might say, but most people could overlook an imaginative four-year-old getting her facts muddled.

Luckily, Zane's only comment was a vague "Austin's nice. And only a couple of hours away. Ever been to the Hill Country before this?"

"No, but I like it here. The people are terrific." She felt warmth rise in her cheeks. Did he know that by "people" she mainly meant him? She wished circumstances were different, that she'd met Zane Winchester in a different time or place. Because she'd grown up without a family of her own, she'd spent *many* hours imagining the family she hoped to one day build— which, naturally, started with a husband. And Zane was the embodiment of all the qualities she admired. Christopher had blindsided her with his charisma and money, like some fairy-tale prince. He could have asked out any girl on campus and his single-minded courtship had made her feel so damn special.

"Alex?" Zane had flipped the switch on the coffee-maker and was regarding her intently. "You okay?"

She pushed away her conflicted feelings about the past, a tangle of regrets intermingled with gratitude that Christopher had given her a beautiful baby girl, and forced herself to focus. "Guess I'm just tired. One cup of coffee, but then we really should be going."

"Deal." After a moment, he resumed his questions about his daughter. "Did Eden happen to mention a boy? Someone she might be interested in?"

She propped her elbows on the kitchen island. "The conversation was more general than that."

"She said something today about if she were going

out with a guy," he told her. "I'm praying it was just a hypothetical statement."

"It may have been. But she is fifteen. You have to accept that those conversations are probably just around the corner. She wants you to treat her as a young woman, not a child."

"Then she has to meet me halfway, start making more mature decisions." He straightened, looking less like a nervous father and more like a seasoned disciplinarian. "These shortsighted rebellions like not completing her work are because she's ticked at Val and me for relocating her. She's better than that."

"True. But if she cleans up her act, demonstrates real progress, would you be willing to consider certain privileges?"

"As long as it doesn't involve boys." He grinned. "None of her other requests could be as nerve-racking as letting her date."

She almost felt sorry for him. "There *was* something special she mentioned before you and Belle returned. She wants to get her learner's permit and take driving lessons."

"My daughter behind the wheel of a car?" A muscle twitched in his jaw. "I don't think so."

"How old were you when you got your permit?" Alex inquired sweetly.

"I— That's different. I was an honors student! And cars were different. Speed limits weren't… The traffic laws have changed."

"Yeah, we all have to wear seat belts now. And more vehicles have air bags than ever before."

He scowled. "Why are you so adamant about her learning to drive?"

"I'm not. I'm just playing devil's advocate, trying to get you to think about all sides of the argument instead of giving her a knee-jerk rejection."

"I'll consider it." He plowed a hand through his hair. "But if she's going to take driver's ed this spring, you have to give me your phone number. I might need you to periodically talk me off the ledge."

With a laugh, she reached for one of the napkins in the ceramic holder on the island. "Got a pen?" She'd just finished scrawling the last digit when she was struck by the impact of what she'd done. Until yesterday, only Bryce had this number. Now she'd given it to Zane and Paul, the festival cashier, and Tess that morning, letting her know that Alex was interested in cultivating a small, select clientele.

She had an urge to crumple the napkin instead of sliding it across the counter to Zane. "I, uh… It's been a long time since a guy asked for my number," she said. She didn't look up, but she could feel him watching her.

"Are you thinking about your husband?" he asked softly.

"Not him specifically. More about how strange it is to be single again." Despite the many things she couldn't confide to Zane, she felt compelled to be as honest as she could. "My husband and I were separated before he died, and the split had been a long time coming. The grief I feel over Chris's death is mostly for the tragedy of it and for Belle, who will grow up without him in her life. It wasn't… I don't mourn him romantically, if that makes sense. Lord, am I sounding like the most heartless woman in the world?"

"No. I understand what you're getting at. I have an ex-wife, remember? I'm not in love with her, but if anything ever happened to her… It can't be easy."

She sniffed, determined not to cry. "Nothing between us was easy. Even in the beginning, when he was sweeping me off my feet, I was nervous, uncertain why he wanted me. With the exception of his parents' disapproval, we had a pretty magical first year of marriage, but then there were the miscarriages. And the longer we were together, the more I realized we had very different life philosophies. I was packed up to leave him when we found out I was carrying…Belle." The name didn't roll off her tongue as smoothly as it should have. She'd been momentarily caught up in the past, forgetting who they were supposed to be in the present.

"Anyway." She tried to refocus. "With the baby on the way, he swore he'd try harder and I needed to believe him. For a few months, it was like a second honeymoon, but fatherhood made him giddy. He seemed to think he was invincible. He took chances that made me cringe and became more reckless with each passing year. After I left, he ended up totaling his car. If I'd been able to help him change…"

"You can't think that way." Zane came around the side of the kitchen island, laying his hand over hers.

"You are not responsible for his death. Just like I'm not responsible for the hundreds of bad choices Val made. I used to think I could 'save' her. I can't decide if I was being arrogant or naive. She is who she is."

"And you let her take Eden?" Alex wasn't trying to judge; she was merely curious. He didn't paint a picture of a stable mother.

He expelled a breath. "Guess I have to live with some bad choices of my own. It really did seem like the right decision at the time, though."

Alex averted her gaze. "As parents, sometimes we just have to do what we think is right at the moment." If he ever learned who she was, would he understand her actions or would he condemn her outright for breaking the law and not trusting the system?

How could she, though, when her husband and father-in-law had so often demonstrated ways to get around that system?

"Coffee's ready," Zane said. "Hey… You're crying?"

She blinked rapidly. "No. Not at all." At least, not yet.

"I'm a terrible host," he said. "I should have let you leave back when you were stuffed with cake and still smiling."

"I'll be all right. Except I'm embarrassed to end the evening on this note." Her eyes stung. She hated that Zane always seemed to see this emotional side of her. Where was a strong protective wall when you needed one? "Belle and I both had a wonder…" She hiccuped, her vision blurring. "Wonderful…"

"Aw, hell. C'mere, honey." Zane wrapped his arms

around her, pulling her into a bear hug against his chest. He was solid and reassuring. And smelled really good. "It'll get better."

"You mean my attempts to interact with people? Because you may be wrong." She smiled weakly against his shirt, her words muffled. "I may be irrevocably socially inept."

"Join the club. I was lucky enough to have dinner with a beautiful woman tonight, and I made her cry."

She glanced up. "Quite the pair, aren't we?"

He met her gaze with a wry smile, but whatever he'd been about to say never made it into the conversation. His expression grew more serious, his eyes more avid. His embrace loosened, one arm sliding down to her waist.

"Alex." The single word held want and apology and frustration.

Her heart fluttered against her ribs. Her body heated with the knowledge that this very attractive man wanted to kiss her. It would be a mistake, of course, and she would pull away before it happened. But the possibility of what it would be like was dizzying.

He stepped back, dropping his arms to his side and once again proving his parents had raised a gallant son. "I should let you go," he said ruefully. "Maybe that coffee isn't such a good idea."

"Maybe not." No matter how hot or delicious it no doubt was. "I'll, uh, get Belle."

Nodding, he put more distance between them, stopping beside her domed cake plate. "Do you want to take the rest of this home?"

"You and Eden keep it. I made it for you." She was congratulating herself on how natural her voice sounded when he caught her gaze again.

"I'll be sure to bring back your dish."

So she'd be seeing him again soon? Damn it.

But, also, less wisely, *yay*.

WERE ALL CHILDREN BORN with an innate sense of when their parents were at their weakest? It had taken Alex a long time to fall asleep after they'd returned from the Winchesters'. And even once she had, her dreams had been restless. She dutifully dragged herself out of bed to fix Belle's breakfast, but she wasn't firing on all cylinders. *Need coffee.* That thought led her right back to Zane, leaving her distracted when Belle once again broached the subject of dance lessons at Tess's studio.

Alex didn't even fully realize she'd agreed until Belle leaped out of her chair with a squeal of joy. *Oh, boy.* On the positive side, the lessons would be good for her daughter. And letting Belle interact with the other little girls seemed a lot less risky in light of the colossal blunder Alex had almost made last night. Nearly kissing an officer of the Texas Department of Public Safety, Ranger Division? She might as well get in the car, drive straight to the Houston courthouse and turn herself in.

After the ballet studio opened for the day, Alex drove her daughter into town to register for classes. Tess was delighted to see them.

"I wasn't sure you'd take me up on my offer," the redhead admitted. "But I'm so glad you did! She has a real flair for showmanship—she'll be a natural on-stage. Her age group meets on Thursdays, so she can still catch this week's class. We sell a limited supply of leotards, but other stores in town have a bigger selection. And of course she'll need shoes."

Alex was sitting on the floor of a department store that afternoon, helping her daughter try on ballet slippers, when the cell phone in her pocket rang. She did a mental run-through of the list of people who had her number, wondering if Bryce had another update for her. Or if Zane had found himself thinking of her today as much as she'd been thinking about him.

But the shy "hello" on the other end belonged to Eden Winchester. "Alex? Hope you don't mind my calling. I wanted to say thank you. Your advice about smiling at the other students and looking more approachable worked."

"Terrific!" *That was fast.* Nice to see Maggie Reardon's long-ago advice was still applicable. "So what happened? You make a new friend?"

"I smiled at a guy in the lunch line, and he and his friend came and sat with me."

Uh-oh. "A guy, huh?"

"Yep. And he's in my math class. He said he could help me with homework sometime."

Your dad's gonna love that. "Well…good for you. I'm proud of you, Eden."

At the teenager's name, Belle lunged for the phone.

"Can I talk to her? I wanna tell her about my new classes and the sparkly skirt we bought and the shoes that make noise."

"Eden, do you have a minute? There's someone here who'd like to say hi."

"Sure, but can I ask you something first? Dad's going out of town to testify in a court case tomorrow and might not be back until late. He thought maybe I could hang out at Beckie's house with her family, but I'm old enough to stay by myself."

"You're not asking me to argue with your dad on your behalf, are you?" Alex had already pushed the boundaries by talking to Zane about his daughter driving. She didn't want to make a habit of getting caught between them.

"No, but I had an idea for a compromise. Would you be willing to check on me, maybe let me eat dinner with you guys? Please! I could have some time alone in the afternoon, then read with Belle and help her get ready for bed or whatever that night. I want to show him he can trust me."

Alex was all too familiar with the adolescent desire to prove herself. She'd gone through a period where she'd thought if she just tried harder, if she was good enough, someone would love her enough to keep her. She sighed, knowing she couldn't say no. "It's all right with me if it's okay with your dad."

"Thanks! You're the best, Alex. I'll have him call you later to officially give his permission. See you tomorrow."

"Here's Belle." As Alex half listened to her daughter share the events of her day, it occurred to Alex that she shouldn't be surprised Eden was already making friends. *After all, just look how fast* my *social circle is expanding.*

IT SEEMED LIKE ONLY SECONDS passed Thursday afternoon between the squeak of school bus brakes at the top of the street and the knock at Alex's front door. She knew Eden was supposed to check in with her, but she hadn't expected the girl to sprint.

"That was quick."

"Guess what!" Eden's cheeks were rosy, her grin contagious. "I got asked to the festival dance!"

Alex's answering smile faltered. "You did? Wh—"

"Eden, Eden, Eden!" Belle kept up the chant as she raced downstairs.

"Hold it, you." Alex shook a finger at her daughter. "First of all, we only use walking feet on the steps. Secondly, Eden has to do homework before she can spend time with you. She'll come back over after she's finished her school assignments and taken Dolly for a walk."

Belle's face fell. "Barnacles!" She'd heard the pseudo-expletive on a cartoon the other day, and it had replaced deduce as her new favorite word. She trudged back to her room, pausing dramatically at the second-story landing for one last woebegone glance.

Eden laughed. "Too bad she's not older. Our theater department could really use her."

"You are the second person this week who's suggested Belle has a future in the performing arts. I just hope she thanks me in her inevitable Oscar speech." Alex hesitated. Although Zane didn't want his daughter procrastinating—Eden was supposed to tackle her homework immediately—surely another ten minutes wouldn't hurt anything. "I realize you're too old for the whole after-school milk-and-cookies routine, but do you want to join me for a snack, maybe tell me more about this dance?"

Eden dropped her backpack in the foyer, not looking at all offended by the maternal offer. "Got anything chocolate?" At the kitchen table, she noticed Alex's frown. "I know what you're thinking."

That your father's going to kill me?

"But this isn't like a car date," Eden continued. "Frederick-Fest comes to a close with a big dance Friday night. Half the town goes. There will be a battle of the bands, they crown a festival princess and junior princess, they'll announce the winners of that chef competition…it's a whole thing with a deal. Leo will be there with his older brother and asked if I'd save him some dances. I just have to convince Dad we should go."

"Good luck with that." Alex sliced through a pan of chocolate chip brownies. "Is Leo the same guy who ate lunch with you the other day, the potential math tutor?"

"Yep, Leo Cochran. He's funny. And sweet." She stared into space, her expression dreamy. "I'll bet he's a good dancer."

Oh, yeah. Zane is definitely going to kill me.

I<small>T WAS ABOUT NINE-THIRTY</small> when Zane turned his truck into the subdivision. How was it that a long day sitting in a courtroom felt more grueling than the hours he'd spent helping a buddy train for a federal fitness test? When he'd first approached Fredericksburg, he'd been bone tired. But the closer he got to home, the more revived he felt.

Perhaps because he was picking up his daughter at Alex's house? He'd received a text earlier in the evening saying that the forecast predicted rainstorms. Even though Eden wanted to demonstrate her growing independence, the howling wind had been freaking her out. He was smiling when he pulled into the Hunt's driveway and knew it wasn't just because he looked forward to seeing Eden. Figuring that Belle was already asleep, he rapped lightly on the door. Alex had probably seen his headlights.

The smiling brunette in a fuzzy blue sweat suit that nearly swallowed her bore little resemblance to the starchy woman he'd first met.

"Hey, there," she greeted him. "Perfect timing. Eden and I just finished our movie."

He followed her into the living room, where Eden was sniffling at the closing credits of an old romantic comedy.

"I thought this film was supposed to be funny," he said, bewildered.

Alex nodded. "It is. But it's touching, too. Want some popcorn?"

"Sure." It was tough to resist the buttery smell. Besides, he was in no hurry to leave. He'd been in the Comers' house dozens of times but the familiar setting now seemed wrong. What would the place look like if it were Alex's? What pictures of her and Belle would adorn the walls?

Alex got the remote from the coffee table and turned off the television. She gently cleared her throat at Eden, who blushed a deeper pink than the streaks in her hair. Obviously, his daughter had something she was reluctant to discuss. Zane's blood pressure rose. More trouble at school? He'd thought they were finally progressing beyond that.

"Something wrong?" he asked, trying not to jump to conclusions.

"Not at all," Alex answered, uncharacteristically chipper. She sat on the sectional couch next to his daughter. "In fact, something fun happened to Eden today. Before she tells you, though, just a reminder that we should keep our voices down—Belle's asleep."

Okay, now he was really worried. If she was concerned about the noise level, why hadn't she just sent them home to have their discussion? Had Eden specifically requested that Alex take part in the conversation? Obviously, he wasn't the only Winchester who knew the strategic value of having backup.

"Is this the driving thing?" he asked. "I'm mulling it over as promised, but it's too soon for a ruling."

Eden didn't meet his gaze. "Actually, Dad, I kinda have something else for you to mull."

Oh, please let it be cider, he thought wearily. "Well,

spit it out. We've inconvenienced Alex enough for one evening."

"You know how the festival closes with a big annual dance?" Eden blurted. "I think you and I should go. Or maybe you could even drop me off." When Alex poked her in the shoulder, Eden grudgingly added, "There's a boy going who I'd like to see."

He dropped his head in his hands. Apparently, his relief earlier in the week that she wasn't interested in any particular boy had been premature.

"I know I'm not allowed to date, per se—"

"Per se?" He didn't think she should date *period*.

"It's not like I'm climbing out my window to meet the guy. We just want to maybe dance a couple of times at a huge public event. No big."

"Eden Jo, don't try to con me. If it was no big deal, you wouldn't have turned red and stammered through the first half of your explanation." Meanwhile, should he be looking into having her bedroom window bolted shut? "Does this kid who wants to make time with my daughter have a name?" *That can be run through a quick background check.*

"Leo Cochran." Eden sighed. "And he's *wonderful*."

"Cochran? Leo Cochran?" Hell, he didn't even need the background check. "I know him. And I don't want you anywhere near him."

"What?" Eden shot to her feet. "Are you kidding?"

He took a deep breath, knowing she was disappointed and confused. "His uncle was arrested last spring, and during initial questioning, Leo lied for him. I'm sorry, Eden, but—"

"Arrested? Leo wouldn't commit a crime. Maybe his uncle's crooked, but Leo's a good guy."

"He lied to the police during an official investigation! You aren't hanging around with someone who has no regard for the truth or the law." When he saw Alex flinch, he realized he must have unintentionally raised his voice.

He started to say they should finish talking about this at home, where there wasn't a four-year-old sleeping, but that would give the misleading impression that the topic was still up for discussion. They were done. Eden was just beginning to show better judgment in the choices she made; he wasn't about to let her spend time with someone who already had one foot down the wrong path.

"Zane…"

He swung his gaze to Alex, warning her mutely not to interfere. This was partly his fault because he'd encouraged the female bonding in the first place. He was glad Eden had a woman she could confide in, but that didn't mean he'd tolerate having his parental decisions contradicted in front of his only child.

"We should go," he told Eden gently. She had a right to be upset, and he didn't expect her to forgive him immediately. He did, however, expect her to respect his authority.

Her bottom lip trembled as she looked to Alex for support.

"Your dad wants what's best for you," Alex murmured, dropping her arm over the girl's shoulder in a sideways hug.

Eden's only response was a rude noise.

Alex walked them to the door on the pretext of showing them out, but she put her hand on Zane's arm once they reached the porch. "Can we talk for a second?"

From the hopeful glance Eden cast back, it was clear she hoped her ally would be able to wear him down. He didn't appreciate the sense that they were ganging up on him. Hadn't he made his position clear?

"It's been a long day," he said gruffly. "I'm exhausted, and I'm lousy company."

"I'll keep it brief," Alex promised.

Already knowing he was going to regret this, he gave her a terse nod. "Eden, go let Dolly out. I'll be right behind you." As his daughter crossed into their yard, he tried to dissuade Alex as politely as possible. "You're a good parent, and I care about you. I hope you know, I value your opinion. But my mind's made up on this."

She bit her lip. "What Leo did was obviously wrong, but he's a kid. Maybe he didn't set out to lie but just got scared. She's been talking about him all evening, and I think he could actually be a good influence on her. She's hoping to ace a math quiz to impress him."

"I'm sure there are students in that school who are good at math and *haven't* lied to the police," Zane said. "I don't want to argue with you, Alex. Let it go." Though his tone was soft, there was no mistaking the steel in his voice. Zane was over six feet tall and carried a Colt .45—he didn't normally have to ask twice to get someone to back down.

But Alex fumed up at him, her eyes shimmering with anger. "You showed up on my porch not long ago talking about rehabilitation and kids making fresh starts. Has Leo done anything since his one past mistake, or have you indicted him because of a single error in judgment? Do you know anything about his recent conduct, or are you too inflexible to consider he might be a good person?"

Zane blinked. "What are you, his lawyer? Why are you taking this so personally?"

The question seemed to deflate her. "I'm not!"

He arched an eyebrow.

"I just believe every story has two sides."

"On that, we agree." He stepped off the porch into the shadows of the yard. "A right side and a wrong one."

Chapter Eight

Walking through the front doors of the high school always gave Zane the weird sensation of being two people at once—the teenager he'd been when he himself attended class here and the proud, anxious, protective father of a teen he was now. Most of the time, his high school days seemed like a previous lifetime. But being inside the building, walking down the same halls, brought the memories so vividly to life he felt as if he should be getting textbooks out of his locker. At a pivotal time in his life, this building had been his second home.

His daughter, on the other hand, probably viewed it as the foreign land to which she'd been exiled.

Ever since Eden's mumbled goodbye as he dropped her off this morning, Zane had been battling an irritating grain of guilt that rubbed him raw like a pebble in his shoe. After all, he'd been the one admonishing her to try harder to fit in and make friends and now that she had… Why did it have to be with that Cochran kid?

Pushing aside Eden's disappointment and the fact that she'd barely acknowledged his existence over breakfast, Zane signed in at the front office visitor log. The vice principal stood behind the counter, waiting for some papers to finish printing. She grinned when she saw him.

"Mr. Winchester, what brings you to see us on a Friday afternoon? Speaking to one of our Texas History classes about the legacy of the Rangers?"

"No, ma'am. Actually I have an appointment with Ms. Peet, the guidance counselor."

The receptionist glanced up from the folders she was filing. "Ms. Peet had to make an emergency phone call to a parent. Would you mind having a seat and waiting? She'll buzz me on the intercom when she's ready."

"Not a problem." Except that sitting in one of the office chairs gave him time to replay the comments other officers had made at lunch today. There'd been some debate, but the prevailing opinion was that he'd overreacted last night.

"I get that you're in a tough spot," Jason Higgs had empathized. "Eden was running wild in California and you're trying to lay down the law. If she'd asked to go to a party with the guy, of course you should have said no! But a chaperoned dance? Where *you're* one of the chaperones?"

"It wasn't the 'where' I had a problem with, it was the 'who.' Can you tell me," he'd challenged Jason, "that you would let your daughter date someone with Leo's background? Someone with ties to a criminal, someone willing to lie to law enforcement?"

Jason had squirmed in his chair. It was easier to be

the voice of reason when you were talking about someone else's child.

But Gina Sandusky had interjected, "She won't always know the guy's background. You know my sister's going to college soon. Don't you hope Eden will go one day, too? Before she's out there on her own, unprotected, you have to give her a chance to hone her own instincts about which guys she can trust and which are creeps."

Zane hadn't thought of it that way.

"Mr. Winchester," the receptionist called out, "the counselor is ready now. You know where her office is?"

"Oh, yeah." Ever since Eden had moved here, Zane and the counselor had become regular buddies.

Today's meeting went more pleasantly than most of their previous ones. Ms. Peet reported that Eden's quiz scores had improved dramatically—indicating that she was paying better attention in class and actually doing her reading at home—and she had caught up on her assignments. She'd stopped shy of accepting two teachers' offers of extra credit projects, but she was certainly meeting the mandatory requirements.

"I know this transition hasn't been easy for you, either," Ms. Peet told him, "and I don't want to force you into the role of bad guy, always nagging her. But if you can get her to consider some of this optional extra work, she may be able to counteract her previous transcripts, make herself more attractive to potential colleges. She still has a couple of years to prove herself. If she puts forth a concerted effort…"

He suddenly recalled Alex's words, that Eden wanted

to excel in math to impress Leo. *Ask yourself this, Winchester. When you were fifteen, which would have provided more significant motivation—a parent badgering you or the chance to show off for a crush?*

"Thank you for your time, Ms. Peet." He stood. "Can I ask you one last question?"

"Of course. That's what I'm here for."

"Do you know Leo Cochran?"

She raised an eyebrow. "I do. But I don't usually discuss specific students with anyone other than their own guardians."

"Right. I get that. I'm not asking for confidential information. I just..." He rocked back on his heels, at a loss.

Ms. Peet pursed her lips. "It's no secret that the head of the math department wants to recruit Leo to represent the school in academic competition next year. And he stays after school sometimes to volunteer as a peer tutor. He's a good kid."

The key word there probably wasn't good so much as kid. For years, Zane had dealt with thugs and kidnappers and drug-runners. Leo Cochran was a teenager—sure, one who had erred in judgment and would probably do so again. But he was a potential *mathlete*, for pity's sake, not a drug lord. Zane would rather Eden learn about relationships here, under his watch, than by following Valerie's example of manic serial-dating.

Zane made it back to the front office just as the final bell rang, releasing students for the weekend. He'd told Eden to meet him there after his appointment. Judging from her slumped posture and inaudible greeting, she wasn't excited to see him.

"I could have taken the bus," she said. "I'm sure you have criminals to track down."

"True. But I hardly got to see you yesterday. I thought we could grab a couple of milk shakes."

She heaved a sigh and he could almost see the cartoon thought bubble over her head—that she wasn't a little girl anymore—but there was no sarcasm in her tone when she agreed, "Sure."

"Or it doesn't have to be shakes. We could, I don't know, go for sushi," he improvised wildly. Was there even a place that served it nearby? To him, sushi had always sounded more like bait he'd hook on the end of a fishing pole than something he'd voluntarily eat. "I just think it would be a good idea to order something and sit at a table where we can discuss rules for the dance tonight."

"You're saying I can go as long as I stay away from Leo." Her bottom lip trembled. "Honestly, I'd rather just stay home."

He smoothed a hand over her hair. "No, sweetheart, I'm saying you can go and this Leo kid better be worth your high opinion of him."

"What? You changed your mind? *You?*" She hurtled toward him—presumably for a hug but with enough energy to execute an NFL-worthy tackle. At the last second, she drew up short and glanced around, obviously recalling their surroundings.

"It's all right," he told her. "You can hug me later."

"Thank you, Daddy." The smile she gave him was so bright it momentarily blinded him. "I won't let you down."

"I appreciate the sentiment, but, even if you let me down from time to time, I still love you. No matter what."

Although her smile hadn't faltered, her gaze had turned watery. Zane was surprised to discover his own eyes stung.

"I think I'll take that milk shake now," she said.

"No sushi?" he teased.

Eden chuckled. "Don't worry, I wouldn't do that to you."

"That's my girl."

Tess raised her voice to be heard above the loud country music. "Have I mentioned how glad I am that you decided to meet me here?"

"Repeatedly," Alex said, "but it's nice to feel appreciated."

"I wish you could've met Lorelei, but she's off on a trail ride this weekend with her hot cowboy."

Probably a good thing—Alex wasn't sure how two more people would have fit into this pavilion. Eden's estimate that "half the town turns out for the closing festivities" had been a conservative understatement. Citizens and tourists of all ages were present, from four-year-old Belle—who had once again donned the rubber duck boots since she didn't actually own cowgirl boots—to a couple in their eighties dressed in coordinated red-and-white square dancing outfits. On the crowded dance floor, a father had his elementary-school-aged daughter balanced on his feet to show her the steps.

Meanwhile back in our neighborhood, a different father and daughter are probably holed up in their house not speaking to each other.

Alex gave herself a mental shake. She was determined not to think about the Winchesters. Her argument with Zane last night had left her troubled. He'd been so unyielding, so unwilling to forgive that boy's deception. The more she dwelled on it, the more upset she got. When Tess had called this morning to see if Alex and Belle planned to attend the community dance, Alex had leaped at the invitation. She needed to get out of the house.

Technically, she needed to get out of her own head for a while, but since that wasn't an option, anesthetizing herself with raucous live music and occasionally swirling around the floor with Belle in her arms was a good substitute. Belle was thrilled to be here. She'd already pointed out several little girls she'd met in yesterday's dance class.

"Mommy, can we dance some more?"

"Actually, they're about to stop the music," Tess said. "They'll announce festival princess results between sets. Although I don't know why they bother with junior princess. That's gone to a Biggins girl since way back when I was in kindergarten with Babs Biggins. Do me a favor, Alex. If you and Belle are around this time next year, could you please enter her? Someone should give the Biggins family a run for their money!"

A few minutes later, the Master of Ceremonies confirmed that this year's junior princess was Julianna Biggins, prompting Tess to roll her eyes. Then they gave the festival princess crown to a young woman named Beckie Sandusky.

"She's lucky," Tess said. "There wasn't a Biggins in the right age range this year to run against her. Oh, there's Farrah Winstead. I should say hi. Want to come meet her?"

"Actually, I think Belle and I are going to hit the concessions table. Thanks, anyway." In the hour that they'd been here, Alex had decided Tess hadn't been exaggerating when she'd said she knew everyone in town. Alex had already been introduced to so many people that her brain was spinning with names. It would be a miracle if she ever managed to attach them to the right faces.

Holding her daughter's hand, Alex led her away from the dance floor and stage, to the comparative peace of the open air. Vendors had started to break down the booths that had dotted the landscape all week, but there were still several groups selling food. She ordered a grilled corn cob even though she suspected she and Belle would end up with butter and paprika all over themselves and a lemon-lime soda for them to share. As she paid for the beverage, she couldn't help recalling Zane's jokes the other night, his offer to open the carbonated beverage and let it breathe.

Get a grip. She was an adult, not a moony teenager.

Was she really going to associate Zane with everything now—sodas, coffee…pickup trucks, just because he drove one? Maybe jeans, because he looked so good in them?

"Mommy, what's wrong?" Belle was peering up at her with concern. "You look sad."

"No, punkin. I'm just mad at myself."

"Did you do something bad?" Belle sounded fascinated by this possibility. "Maybe you need to be in time-out."

Too bad Alex couldn't share her daughter's simplistic view of how the world worked. "You about done with that corn? They've started playing music again if you'd like to dance."

The girl bobbed her head in agreement. "Miss Tess says I am 'a natural talent.'"

As they neared the pavilion, Alex scooped her daughter into her arms so she wouldn't lose her in the throng. They jostled their way toward the dance floor, staying on the perimeter rather than wading into the crowd. Alex knew her arms would get too tired to hold Belle for many songs in a row, so she poured all her energy into spinning Belle around as much as possible for this one lively number. The band was winding down for a ballad when Belle's eyes suddenly rounded in surprise.

"Mommy! It—"

A hand tapped Alex's shoulder. "Ladies. May I cut in?" Zane asked. He was clean-shaven and looked great in a pair of black jeans and a deep green button-down shirt. "I was hoping Miss Belle would do me the honor of a dance."

Alex tried to recover from her shock at seeing him here. "Where's *your* daughter?"

His lips compressed into a thin line. "Dancing with Leo Cochran, I imagine. After a lot of careful consideration, I decided maybe he isn't public enemy number one. And if they're going to be friends, I'd just as soon they get to know each other somewhere I can keep an eye on them."

"Makes sense."

He held her gaze. "I do believe in fresh starts, you know. And it seemed hypocritical to want one for my daughter, then act as if no one else deserves them. What do you say, can Belle and I have that dance?"

"Absolutely." Alex walked to the sidelines, watching her daughter enjoy Zane's attention. Should she take hope in the fact that he was willing to give Leo a second chance? If he ever learned the truth about Alex, would he give her a chance to explain? Granted, she was a grown woman, not an intimidated teenager, but there had been extenuating circumstances.

"If I'd known Zane was going to show up looking for dance partners," Tess announced as she sidled up to Alex, "I would have stayed close to you guys. Your daughter is really aptly named—Belle of the ball, indeed. Some kids turn out to be such a perfect match for what they're called. Do you think the names they're given help shape their personalities, or do you think those personalities were evident from the get-go, shaping parents' choices?"

"I, uh, never gave it much thought. My husband and I used a family name." Specifically, his aunt Josephine's.

"Want to know my shameful secret? My name is actually Contessa. Contessa Gretchen Fitzpatrick." She made a face. "What a horrible thing to do to a defenseless baby. My older sister is Regina, which means 'queen.' Our mother wanted royalty. Instead, she got me."

"Trust me, as shameful secrets go, that one's not so bad. Contessa's…unique."

"Oooh. Don't look now." Tess's voice became hushed, almost reverent. "But I think it's your turn."

Alex followed her friend's gaze and saw Zane headed toward them, carrying Belle piggyback style.

"If he asks you to dance," Tess coached, "your answer is yes. I'll watch Belle. I promise not to take my eyes off of her." She'd heard about the girl's nerve-racking disappearance at the festival. "And I'll hold your purse, but you have to extend me the same courtesy if a guy who looks like that ever wants to cut a rug with me."

When Zane reached them, he lowered Belle to the ground and exchanged hellos with Tess. Then his gaze swung to Alex. "Waltz with me?" The new song was faster than the previous ballad but definitely three-four time.

"All right."

The teenager Alex had once been—gangly and afraid of making mistakes—had never danced. But early in her marriage it had become clear she would be attending a number of formal functions each year, so she'd taken some lessons. This wasn't a ballroom waltz, though. Zane's movements were fluid and less predictable. It took her a few measures to abandon the programmed preciseness of her steps and simply follow his lead.

The music washed over her, and the people around them fell away. She let her head rest against Zane's shoulder. This was the third time she'd been in his arms. Every time she found herself here, it grew more difficult to remember why she shouldn't kiss him.

"Alex?" His voice was a husky murmur. She wouldn't even have heard him over the band if she hadn't been pressed against him. "I'm sorry for last night. I'm entitled to make decisions regarding my daughter, but I shouldn't be an ass about it."

"You weren't an ass. She *is* your daughter, and you'd just finished a very long drive. All things considered, you were fairly patient." Her mouth curved in a smile. "Wish I could've seen her face when you told her you'd changed your mind. She's probably already working on her essay to nominate you as father of the year."

"I didn't change my mind completely. I just decided to give the kid a chance on a probationary basis." His muscles stiffened beneath her hands as he glared across the room. "Probation or not, though, if he wants to get through the night alive, he shouldn't be holding my daughter so close."

She stifled a laugh.

"My paternal angst is funny to you?" he growled.

"Not exactly. It just struck me as ironic, you complaining that they're dancing too close when you and I are…" She tilted her face up, meeting his gaze.

"Not nearly close enough," he said.

Heat rose within her. "Zane." Her mouth was dry. She swallowed and tried again. "I don't—"

"I know. Not here. Your kid's watching. My kid's in sight. Hell, even my parents are here."

"They are?" She probably should have expected that but, not having family of her own, it wasn't the type of thing that occurred to her.

He cupped her chin and looked her straight in the eye. "Even with all these witnesses around, even knowing this isn't the time or place, I still want to kiss you."

Her stomach did a triple somersault. Her head swam with a pleasant dizziness that made it hard to think, much less answer.

"Big finish," he said.

"What?" But he'd already begun to spin her. Then, as the song came to an end, he dipped her.

It wasn't until they'd stopped dancing and he let go of her that she slowly regathered her wits. "Zane, your interest is flattering. And I admit, I'm very attracted to you. But…there's a lot you don't know about me."

"I'd like to learn," he said.

That's what I'm afraid of.

"Ladies and gentleman, may I have your attention please!"

"Now what?" Alex asked. "How many princesses do you people have at this thing?"

"Different announcement," Zane said as they reached Tess and Belle. "This is for the cooking competition that's going to be shown on cable."

Tess bounced lightly on the balls of her feet. "Oh, I'm so nervous for Grace! Alex, have you been to the Jalapeño yet? Great food."

Alex shook her head. On stage, the TV show's host Damien Craig, was being introduced. He outlined the prizes for which the chefs had been competing and re-capped the finalists—Katharine Garner, Ty Beckett, Reed Lockhart and Grace Torres. "We thank you for your participation in our contest," Damien said. "A lot of you voted over the past week, and those results were added to the judges' scores. It was a tough call, but ear-lier today a winner was decided. And that winner is… Chef Ty Beckett!"

The applause around them didn't completely drown out Tess's heartfelt "Damn."

Belle looked up, an admonishing expression on her pixie features. "That's a bad word. You should say 'bar-nacles' instead!"

"You're right," Tess agreed repentantly. To Alex, she added, "Sorry, it just slipped out."

"Don't worry, it happens." She didn't share with her friend that Chris used to think it was funny to teach their daughter inappropriate phrases. Alex had tried various lines of reasoning to get him to stop. *What ex-actly am I supposed to say down the road when I start getting calls from her principal?* Chris had scoffed that when juxtaposed with a big donation to the school's library or music department, a few swearwords wouldn't bother anyone.

Alex realized that Zane was waving at someone across the pavilion. "Eden and her young suitor?" she asked.

He shook his head. "Mom and Dad. I should catch up with them, commiserate about the parental torture of having your teenager date. They'll appreciate the karmic payback after the fits I gave them."

"You?" Alex asked disbelievingly. "I wouldn't have pictured you as a wild child."

"I wasn't, but I fell for one. They tried to accept Valerie while we were married, but she was never who they would have chosen for me."

Neither am I.

"Would you and Belle like to meet them?" he offered.

"Another time," she lied, hoping to postpone an introduction indefinitely. From the way he'd described them, they were upstanding civic heroes. It was bad enough she couldn't be honest with Zane and his daughter. She couldn't face the couple who'd raised him to be such a decent man. "Interacting with other people's parents has always been a little outside my comfort zone," she added truthfully.

In her younger years, she'd dreaded meeting other people's moms and dads because small talk usually led to well-meaning questions about her own family. When Christopher had first introduced her to his parents, she'd been so nervous she'd broken out in hives. It hadn't helped that Eileen spent the entire conversation verbally shredding her in a futile attempt to dissuade Christopher from marrying her.

"Is that your phone?" Tess asked suddenly, looking around to locate the source of sound.

"Oh, I guess it is. You must have better hearing than me." Alex fumbled through her purse. "Hello?"

"Hey, Red."

"H-hey." She shot nervous glances at Zane and Tess, as if they could somehow overhear the call—which was ridiculous. Given the decibel level in the pavilion, s*he* could barely hear Bryce. To better block out the din, she covered her opposite ear with her hand. "Can you give me a minute to get someplace quieter and call you back?"

"Sure thing."

"This has been fun," Alex said as she put her phone away. "But Belle and I need to go."

"Everything okay?" Zane asked.

She gave him a strained smile. "If we stay out too late, we turn into pumpkins. But I'll see you soon. You, uh, still have my cake plate. Tess, thanks for your help wrangling the little one."

The fact that Belle didn't object to going home demonstrated how tired she was. Even if Bryce hadn't called, Alex would have needed to leave soon.

"How far away are you parked?" Zane wanted to know. "I can walk you to your car."

"No!" She needed to call Bryce back immediately, find out if that investigator had returned and whether he might even now be reporting her whereabouts to his employers. "With the streetlights and all the people out tonight, that's not necessary. I don't want to cut into your time with your parents."

"All right. Drive safely." He startled her by leaning forward to press a kiss to her forehead. Then he did the same with Belle. Alex noticed the way Tess's eyebrows shot up and knew the dance teacher would be calling her soon.

By the time Alex jogged the two blocks to her car, her calves burned and Belle was getting heavy. She buckled the little girl into her booster seat. From past experience and Belle's sleepy expression, she knew her daughter would be out like a light long before they reached the house.

She dialed Bryce. "Took me a few minutes to get away. Everything okay?"

"Calm down. It's not an emergency," he assured her.

Her immediate reaction was relief, but she cautioned herself not to get complacent. The absence of an emergency right at this moment was no guarantee on the future. "I've been meaning to call you," she said. She'd given this a lot of thought but hated to ask Bryce for more favors. He'd already done too much for her, but if she was going to be proactive about trying to keep her in-laws at bay, she would need a loan. And a point person. "I have to talk to you about something."

"Okay, but me first," Bryce said. "I have juicy news to report. Your mother-in-law, Eileen Hargrove? According to all reports, the lady is coming seriously unglued."

That didn't sound at all like the chilly, poised society matron. "What do you mean?"

"Well, ever since that P.I. knocked on my door, I've been doing some subtle investigation of my own. Nothing overt, just monitoring news items, making casual conversation with acquaintances who've been at any mutual social events. From everything you've told me, Eileen's a viper, but she maintains a certain image."

"Right." She cut her eyes to Belle in the rearview mirror, confirming that the little girl was fast asleep in her car seat. "She's evil, but no one could ever accuse her of confusing a salad fork with a dinner fork."

"Don't be so sure. There are pictures of her at an arts fundraiser last week where she looks pretty bedraggled. A society blogger hinted that Eileen spent more time at the open bar than in the gallery. And she got into an argument with her husband outside the Houston ballet that devolved into a screaming match before the car was brought around. From the snippets I was able to piece together, she might have been ranting about you."

Alex's stomach twisted. Until now, she'd hoped the Hargroves' tendency toward discretion would help shield her from scrutiny. They were very selective about the attention they drew to themselves and had reasons for not wanting the police involved in their lives. But if Eileen's grief over losing her son and fury over losing her granddaughter had resulted in her becoming unhinged and unpredictable, she might come after them more aggressively.

"This is bad," she said softly.

"There's another way to look at it, Red. You said yourself that your late husband was prone to self-destructive behavior. Given time, his mother's behavior might become detrimental enough that no sane judge would let her near Little Red."

"Maybe." She couldn't just sit here hoping for that to happen, though. "Crossing my fingers that she shows her true colors publicly isn't really a plan. I've been working on something else." She told him about the notebook she'd slowly been filling with anecdotal evidence. For instance, there had been a minor government official she'd seen at the Hargrove house on numerous occasions—always either closeting himself in the study with Phillip or quickly leaving—who'd never once approached Phillip and Eileen when they'd all been at the same functions. Why hide their association?

"I think there might be some damning information in that notebook," she said, "but it's not hard evidence. I'd need someone to use my data as a starting point for unearthing more."

"Want to mail it anonymously to the police?" Bryce asked.

She shuddered. "And give them reason to possibly come looking for me? It's obvious those observations come from inside the family, and the Hargroves' only child is dead. I can't draw attention to myself while it's only a woman on the run's word against two pillars of the community. Once I have real proof, then I can go to the authorities. The problem is, I can't currently afford a private investigator to dig for that proof."

"You need me to fund the investigation? Cool. I feel like a behind-the-scenes superhero."

His joking didn't eliminate her guilt. "I wouldn't ask for a loan if it wasn't my daughter at stake. I hope you know that."

"You'd be a terrible mother if you put your pride before the well-being of your child! Besides, I've freely offered to give you money before," he reminded her.

Her gratitude was almost too vast to put into words. "Bryce… You're like our guardian angel."

"I'd rather be your avenging angel. You finish working on that diary of suspicious characters and activities, I'll start researching investigators. Let's take the Hargroves down once and for all."

Chapter Nine

Zane sat in the recliner, flipping through channels in an aimless search for any kind of ball game. But his mind wasn't on the Saturday-afternoon programming. He kept thinking about the way Alex had looked last night—alluring as she'd smiled up at him on the dance floor, frightened when she'd announced it was time to go. Who had been on the other end of that phone?

It wasn't any of his business, yet the question nagged at him because she'd gone pale after she'd answered. He was starting to realize just how many questions he had about Alex. Having lived in this area his entire childhood and most of his adult life, he knew the people in his community quite well. So it was disconcerting to be falling for a near stranger.

Behind him, Eden entered the adjoining kitchen, humming the country song he and Alex had waltzed to last night. Or, as Eden probably thought of it, the country song to which and she Leo had danced.

"Thinking about your date?" he asked.

"Um…" She opened the refrigerator. "Do you know

if we have any sour cream in here? I want to make dip to go with my potato chips."

"I don't think there's any sour cream, but we've got some milk that's probably gone bad. Isn't that roughly the same thing?"

She groaned. "Spare me your attempts at humor, Dad." After rummaging around in the fridge for a few seconds, she reported, "We're out of practically everything."

"Sorry. Guess the last time I did any real grocery shopping was when Alex and Belle came over for dinner."

Eden came into the living room and sprawled across the sofa, her expression wistful. "I wish Alex hadn't left so early last night. I wanted her to meet Leo. She didn't even say goodbye."

"She had to take an important phone call."

Was that the only reason she'd exited so quickly, or had he pushed her away by being too candid? She'd said only earlier this week how bizarre it felt to be single again. What if she wasn't ready to date yet? *You shouldn't have told her you wanted to kiss her.* But it was Zane's nature to be direct. Had he come on too strong and flustered her into retreat?

Maybe he should take her cake plate back and see how she reacted. Of course, if she needed time and space to adjust to the growing attraction between them, showing up on her doorstep might not be the best tactic.

"Hey, Dad? I was thinking I might call Mom tonight."

"That's a great idea," he encouraged. It would be the first time since Eden had been sentenced to Texas that she'd voluntarily initiated conversation with her mother. "Want to tell her about Leo?"

Eden's cheeks turned pink. "Maybe." Then she smirked. "Or maybe I just want to tell her about how *you're* finally dating someone."

"Alex and I are not dating." If Alex was feeling pressured, the last thing she needed was people saying they were in a relationship.

"You're not?" Eden scrunched up her face in a confused frown. "But you cook her dinner and go dancing with her. How do you old people define a date?"

At that, he leaned forward to grab a decorative pillow from the end of the couch and flung it at her.

Eden covered her head, laughing. "Child abuse!"

"No, I'm just following the letter of the law. They're called *throw* pillows. I don't want to get fined for not using them correctly."

His daughter shot him a mischievous grin. "In that case…" She launched two in rapid succession then, realizing she'd given him all the ammo, fled the room shrieking. He was about to toss them after her when the phone rang.

"Hello?"

"It's Ben. Am I calling at a bad time?" The officer didn't sound like his normally gregarious self.

"I was just channel-surfing and considering ordering a pizza. What's up?"

"I need a distraction. Grace is destroyed over losing

that cooking competition. Although, if you ask me, it's more than the contest that's got her upset. I think she got a little too close to one of her opponents. I called to try to cheer her up, but Amy told me neither of them wants to speak to me. Then she hung up."

"Ouch. You want to come over here, have some pizza with me and Eden, maybe play some Xbox football? You owe me a rematch."

"That might work. I still can't drive, but Vic's going to visit Mom at the senior center tonight. He could drop me off and pick me up. We'll pick up a six-pack on the way."

Thirty minutes later, Zane took the aluminum cans so that his friend could better maneuver with his crutches. "*This* is your idea of a six-pack, diet cola? Very manly."

Ben gave him a wounded look. "You have an impressionable young lady under your roof. And, after the last month of hobbling around and not being able to exercise, I've, uh, put on a few pounds. My sister's a chef," he added defensively. "Her answer to trauma is food."

The reminder of Grace's predicament put an end to Zane's teasing. "You think she's going to be okay? She may not have gotten first place, but she's a hell of a chef."

"I know. This was just really crap timing. She's still recovering from losing Dad and Mom's Alzheimer's is getting worse. If the restaurant goes under, too…" Ben shook his head.

They got Ben and his crutches situated, and the pizzas arrived shortly thereafter. Eden hung out with them while they played their video football, alternately cheering them on and heckling them. Eventually, she excused herself to call her mom on the West Coast.

"Looks like you're making progress with her," Ben commented after Eden left the room. "Good for you. I couldn't help notice at the festival dance that you might be making progress on the dating front, too. Who was the curvy brunette?" He whistled, adding something in Spanish under his breath.

"Alex. Watch how you talk about her—I'd hate to beat a man with his own crutches."

"Touchy." Ben grinned.

"Shut up and kick."

"Wait…Alex. Alex Hunt. You asked me about her once. She's lives next to you, right?"

"Yeah." *For now.*

"Convenient. How does Eden feel about her dad making new friends?"

"She loves Alex and her little girl. Eden would be all for it if I asked her out."

"If?" Ben echoed. "You mean you haven't yet? Much as I appreciate our friendship, there are better ways to spend your Saturday nights than playing Xbox with me."

"You don't say," Zane drawled. "I'm trying to move at a respectful speed. She lost her husband in a car accident."

"Oh." Ben sobered immediately. "How long ago was that?"

"A year, give or take. I didn't press for details." On screen, the ref called a delay of game because Zane's center hadn't bothered to hike the ball. There were actually a lot of details he and Alex had never discussed. She'd mentioned an obnoxious neighbor in college, but he had no idea what university she'd attended or what she'd studied. When her husband had been alive, had she worked outside the home or been a housewife? What did she and Belle plan to do once their house-sitting assignment for the Comers ended?

Then again, Alex had entrusted him with some of the most personal details of her life—her childhood in foster homes, her troubled marriage and difficulty having a baby. Those experiences were what had shaped her into a compassionate survivor, a woman who adored her daughter and was willing to help him bridge the gap with his own daughter. Maybe he didn't know what kind of music she preferred or her favorite color, but he knew what mattered.

And he knew that after only a couple of weeks, he was half-crazy about her and that his feelings escalated every time he saw her.

"Yo, you still playing or did you give up?" Ben challenged. "I know I'm tough to beat, but if you're gonna be in the game, be *in* the game. Give it your all."

Zane pointed a finger at his friend. "You're right! You're absolutely right." Alex was only here temporarily, and every moment he ignored his feelings, kept his distance, was a lost opportunity. He'd spent today second-guessing himself, wondering if it had been a mistake to say he wanted to kiss her. His real regret should be that he hadn't just done it. He should have kissed her, then let *her* decide if she was ready to date. His conjecture about what she might be feeling was pointless.

"What time is your brother picking you up?" Zane asked, trying not to sound impatient. It was time to start seizing opportunities.

BELLE HAD BEEN ASLEEP FOR about an hour when she woke from her nightmare. Alex was in the master bedroom, hemming a pair of her daughter's pants when she heard a muffled cry.

She flipped on the hall light as she hurried toward the girl's room. "Are you okay, punkin?"

Her daughter was upright, huddled into the corner with a teddy bear. She'd started to cry. "Had a bad dream."

"About what?" Alex sat on the edge of the bed and held her arms open. Belle snuggled against her, warm from sleep.

"I'm scared."

Alex stroked her hair. "Of what?"

"I want Daddy."

The soft pitiful statement clawed at Alex's heart. She'd never discouraged Belle from talking about Christopher, but she herself rarely brought him up in conversation. It had been a long time since Belle had mentioned him directly, which Alex had chosen to see as a sign of healing. Now she worried that her daughter had simply been repressing her pain. *I should be mentioning him more, encouraging her to talk about her memories.*

"I'm sure your Daddy would have wanted to be here with you. He loved you very much."

"I don't like that he went to heaven," Belle complained.

"I don't either, honey. But sometimes things happen that we just can't understand." She'd never understood Chris's reckless impulses—he'd been an intelligent man, so why the hell couldn't he work through the logical consequences of his actions? Being rich hadn't made him immortal.

"Is Mister Zane going to be my new daddy?"

"What? No! I... He's just our friend."

"Oh." Belle rubbed her nose. "If he was my new daddy, Eden could be my sister. And I'd finally have a dog."

Alex drew a deep breath. "Belle, you know we're not staying here forever, right? We're not moving in with Mr. Zane. He's just going to be our neighbor for a little while."

"Will he still be our neighbor on my birthday?" That was only a couple of weeks away now.

"Yes."

"Can he come to my party?"

"Absolutely."

"Can he get me a dog?"

"Only a stuffed one. We're not ready for a pet."

"*I* am."

Alex chuckled. "I think it's time for you to go back to bed now. Okay?"

Belle nodded, scooting down beneath the covers. "Leave the hall light on, please."

"Deal."

"Mommy?"

"What, punkin?"

"Don't go to heaven."

Alex caught her breath, not sure how to respond. The temptation was to make promises no person could absolutely keep. Why was being a parent so hard? "I love you. I will always, always love you."

"Love you, too, Mommy."

The bittersweet pang in her midsection stayed long after Belle's breathing evened out and she slept once again. *Nobody is taking her from me. Ever.*

The night before, Alex had fallen asleep to satisfying fantasies of discrediting the Hargroves. Writing in her notebook each night before bed, imagining being free of them once and for all, was soothing. It was a shame she hadn't thought to chronicle names and dates when she and Chris were still married, when she was trying to keep the peace as much as possible, but better late than never. She took the notebook out of the otherwise-emptied nightstand drawer, but the pen she'd last used wasn't there. She dumped her purse on the bedspread and was sorting through the contents when she thought she heard a voice.

Wondering if Belle might need her again, she paused, listening intently—then jumped about a foot when something struck her window.

"Alex."

Was she going crazy, or was that Zane? She quickly turned off the bedroom light so she wouldn't be visible, then crept to the window to peek. Seeing that it really was Zane, she opened her window.

"Oh good." He sounded as if he was smiling, although there wasn't enough light to make out his actual expression. "You're awake."

She waited for some kind of explanation as to why he was throwing pebbles at her window—something she'd seen in countless movies but had never experienced in real life—but he didn't offer an immediate reason for why he'd scared her out of her skin and risked waking Belle. If he'd needed to talk, why hadn't he just called?

"Have you been drinking?" she accused. It seemed slightly less insulting than *have you lost your mind?*

"Yes, ma'am. The hard stuff, too. Diet soda *with caffeine.*"

Okay. So he actually had lost his mind. "What are you doing here, Zane?"

"Brought your cake plate." He held up the domed dish.

She could tell him to return it during daylight hours, but why? He was already here, and, truthfully, she was glad to see him. Especially when he was endearingly playful, not glowering while he lectured civilians on the importance of the law. It was ironic that current circumstances placed them on opposite sides of the matter when she had always admired the very qualities Zane epitomized. How many times had she fought with Chris over his disrespect of the rules?

"Be right down," she called. It wasn't until she was unlocking the front door that she realized she'd already scrubbed off her makeup for the day and that she'd removed her bra an hour ago. She was wearing a polka-dotted, short-sleeved baby-doll pajama top over a pair of matching dotted capris. Maybe if she didn't turn on the foyer light, her braless state wouldn't be noticeable. "Evening."

"Nice jammies." The way he drank in the sight of her transformed teasing words into a heady compliment. He handed over the plate. "It's a beautiful night. Want to step out and look at the stars with me?" The innocuous offer didn't quite match the man making it. Wearing a white T-shirt, jeans and a wicked smile, he looked like the kind of guy a girl's mother would warn her about.

But I didn't have a mother. She set the plate in the foyer and stepped outside. "Only for a minute, though. Belle's having a restless night."

Overhead, stars crowded the sky, sparkling in timeless majesty. A breeze rippled over her and she shivered.

"Cold?" Zane stepped behind her, not quite embracing her but sharing the heat of his body. It was tempting to lean back into his chest and melt against him. "Do you know many of the constellations?"

"Nope. On a good day, I can find the Big Dipper. Beyond that..."

"Over there is the Flying Fish." When he raised his hand to point, he brushed her bare arm, causing another slight tremor. Would he attribute it to the night chill, or did he know better? "And you see those two stars?"

He drew a straight line in the air. "Canis Minor. Better known as the little dog."

She gave him a disbelieving look. "Are you just making this up as you go along?"

"Of course not. I was a Scout until the seventh grade."

"But that's not a dog! It's barely enough stars to qualify as a constellation."

"You have to use your imagination. It's probably easier for me because my imagination's been getting a lot of exercise lately." He traced his hand up her arm, slowly and deliberately this time. When he got to her shoulder, he gently turned her to face him. He placed his finger on her lower lip. "I've been imagining this. A lot."

He bent his head to hers, his mouth replacing his finger. Her nerves thrummed, her skin tingled. His tongue slid between her lips, and he kissed her with excruciating tenderness, tasting her thoroughly but slowly, as if he wanted to do this all night. Need unfurled inside her. It had been a very long time since she'd been truly aroused, and she almost gasped at the piercing sweetness of returning desire.

But then Zane pulled away. Smiling, he ran his thumb over the curve of her lip one last time. "Sweet dreams, Alex."

As he sauntered toward his house, she could hear him whistling lightly. *Sweet dreams*? There was no chance in hell she could sleep after that.

ALTHOUGH ALEX WAS UP WITH the sun and the birds, she forced herself to wait until a respectable hour before she called Tess. "Do you have lunch plans today?" she asked the other woman. "Because I desperately need a second opinion."

They settled on a fast-food place that had an indoor playground for Belle and met at noon.

As Belle entertained herself by repeatedly going down a giant spiral slide, Tess sat on the other side of the lime-green booth snickering.

"You find my anxiety funny?" Alex asked.

"It's amusing that *you* wanted to have lunch, but you haven't eaten two bites of your salad. I don't really understand the anxiety. Zane's a great guy and, from what you said, a great kisser. Count your blessings, woman."

That was easy for Tess to say, when she knew so little about Alex's troubles.

Alex swirled her straw around in her drink. "You don't think it's weird that he showed up at my house in the middle of the night, kissed me once, then left?" If he'd been as turned on as she'd been, shouldn't it have been far more difficult for him to go?

"I think it's romantic. Classy, like a single red rose. The question you should be asking is, when's it going to happen again? Are you going to call him today? Arrange an accidental-on-purpose neighbor meeting, like both of you walking to your mailboxes at the same time?"

"It's Sunday. There is no mail. Also, I'm not a stalker."

"You're missing my point. I suppose you could do nothing—wait and see if he shows up again, but that seems a bit passive. I'm not a fan of passive. I'm more of a *doer*."

Alex grinned. "No kidding. I—"

"Heather!"

Oh, God, no. Her head whipped around—an involuntary reflex even as she realized she should be slouching farther down in the booth and trying to hide, though it was too late for that. Shock and dread choked her.

A tall blonde with patrician features and an angry scowl was stalking toward her but veered left long before she got close to their table. "Heather, how many times have I told you to stop pushing your brother!"

Not me. Alex's hands trembled, and nausea roiled through her stomach. *She wasn't talking to me.*

"Alex?" Tess was staring at her as if she'd grown another head.

"Sorry. That woman startled me when she yelled. Here I was lost in thought about Zane, then boom." The explosion reference was entirely too appropriate. She had a sick feeling that at any moment, her life could blow up in her face. What if she'd been here today with Zane? She didn't think he'd be as easily fooled by her lame explanation as Tess. Although Alex should be glad her friend seemed to buy her excuse, she was too ashamed. She hated lying to someone who'd been so kind to her.

She cleared her throat, feigning a sudden interest in their surroundings so she wouldn't have to look Tess in the eye. "Belle's birthday is coming up soon. Think she'd like to have a party here?"

"Nah, you don't want to have it in a place that's open to the public, trying to celebrate in the middle of unsupervised hooligans and brothers and sisters pulling hair and pushing each other. What about the dance studio? If you can be flexible about the time, we can schedule something fun when there's not a class going on. If the birthday girl is open to that idea."

"Are you kidding? She'll be over the moon. Thanks, Tess. I don't deserve you." Alex sipped her sweet tea. It tasted like self-loathing.

So MUCH FOR NOT BEING *a stalker.* On the pretext of using sidewalk chalk to draw with her daughter in the driveway, Alex had kept one eye on the Winchester house all afternoon. She knew it was Zane's routine to walk the dog, and she needed to talk to him. Part of her thought it would be easiest to pretend last night had never happened, but denial was just another form of deception. She already had too much of that on her plate.

She'd almost given up hope on her plan when, finally, Belle shouted, "Hi, Mister Zane!"

He obligingly brought Dolly over so that Belle could pet her. But he barely spared a glance for child or dog. His gaze was locked on Alex. "Hi."

She rose, dusting chalk dust off her jeans. "Belle, can you finish our castle? I want to talk to Mister Zane for a minute."

"Uh-oh." His tone was light, but his eyes were searching, trying to read Alex's expression. "Sounds like I'm in trouble, Belle."

"You have to say you're sorry and go to time-out," the girl said sagely. "Those are the rules."

Alex walked to the end of the driveway. Zane joined her there, keeping his voice down.

"Are you angry about last night?" he asked.

"No." She couldn't stop herself from admitting, "That was a hell of a kiss. But…I don't know what you expect from me. What happens now?"

"That's up to you. You've been through a lot, and I'm a patient man."

Why did he have to be so wonderful? She wanted to cry. "Zane, I like you." She laughed hollowly. "What's *not* to like? You know Belle and I aren't staying, though."

"The Comers are really good people." He scowled. "But I am not looking forward to their coming back. We still have months before then. Why don't we just see what happens? Go out with me. Please."

"I…" The yearning to say yes bubbled up inside her. Her past was a series of bumpy roads that had never quite led where she'd expected; who knew what her future held? Didn't she deserve whatever small bit of happiness she could find? *Doesn't Zane deserve a woman who's honest with him?* "I don't know."

"I realize it would be your first date since Chris died."

"Chris?" Her heart raced. How had he known that?

Zane frowned. "Am I misremembering his name?"

"N-no, you got it right." When had she used his name? Perhaps when she'd told Zane about her husband's accident? She'd obviously slipped somewhere, and it was those tiny mistakes that made spending time with Zane hazardous. "It's just…disorienting to hear you talk about him." That, at least, was the unvarnished truth.

"Anyway, if it helps, don't look at an evening out as some kind of milestone. It's just one night, a few hours in the scheme of things. You can give yourself one night. Give yourself a chance to see what it could be like between us."

Her throat tightened with emotion. If she didn't end this conversation quickly, she'd either capitulate or start crying. Possibly both. "I'll think about it. That's all I can give you at the moment."

"Then I'll take it." He brushed his knuckles over her cheek. "For now."

Chapter Ten

"Excuse me? Alex?"

Alex stood at the front desk of the senior living complex, where she'd been checking in for an appointment with one of the residents. Satisfied client Mrs. Turlow had a friend who lived here and wanted to talk to Alex about restoring a tattered family quilt.

As soon as Alex turned to face the stranger who'd addressed her, she knew who it was. The elderly woman had Zane's green eyes and Eden's smile.

"I *did* overhear you say your name was Alex Hunt?" Zane's mother verified.

"Yes, ma'am."

"How serendipitous! I've been wanting to meet you. Dorothea Winchester." She extended her hand and shook Alex's with a good strong grip. Then she knelt down to beam at Alex's daughter. "And you must be Belle. My granddaughter Eden told me about you."

At the mention of her idol, Belle lit up. "You know Eden? She's my friend! I want pink hair like hers."

"Maybe when you're older," Alex said.

"Five is older," Belle reasoned. "I'll be five soon."

"Older than five."

Dorothea chuckled. "What brings the two of you to Gunther Gardens on a Wednesday afternoon?"

"A potential customer," Alex said. "I do some seamstress work. Belle is going to color *quietly* while I meet with Mrs. Melburne. Isn't that right, Belle?"

"Yes, ma'am."

"Nice to meet you," Alex said awkwardly. "I should really—"

"Can I buy you a cup of coffee?" Dorothea asked. "After you talk to Mrs. Melburne. We have a lovely cafeteria here with all-day bakery selections. They have fantastic c-o-o-k-i-e-s," she added with a glance at Belle.

"That's very thoughtful, but—"

"Wait until I tell my husband, Fred. This will perk him right up! It was such a bitter winter, and he wound up with pneumonia. It dragged on for weeks! He's better now, but his energy's still not at one hundred percent. He couldn't even make it through a whole song with me at the dance last Friday." She tapped her lips, looking distracted. "Maybe it would've helped if I hadn't picked such a fast number. He'll be excited to hear we finally get to meet the mysterious Alex Hunt."

Shoot. Was she really going to disappoint Zane's charming mother and the recuperating Fred?

Alex smiled in spite of herself. "You know, you remind me a lot of your son, Mrs. Winchester." *I have trouble saying no to him, too.*

THE FRESH-BAKED COOKIES in the cafeteria did not disappoint. Alex mustered her self-discipline to keep from going back for a second white-chocolate-cranberry-macadamia-nut square.

"My son's mentioned you several times over the last couple of weeks," Dorothea said. "We were sorry to hear we'd just missed you at the festival dance."

"I had to get Belle home to bed," she said, feeling guilty anew for having weaseled her way out of meeting the Winchesters. They were every bit as good-hearted and decent as she'd expected after hearing Zane talk about them. "Zane speaks so highly of you both. I understand you were a fireman, Mr. Winchester?"

"Call me Fred." He turned to Belle. "Have you ever seen a fire truck up close? I still have some buddies at the station. Maybe you could visit sometime."

Belle leaned forward eagerly. "Don't all fire stations have those spotted dogs?"

"Dalmatians? Not these days. But they used to."

"She loves dogs," Alex said. "In fact, that's how we met Zane. Dolly introduced us."

"Want to meet one right now?" Fred asked. "If that's okay with your mama, of course. My bridge partner lives on this floor and he has a friendly long-haired chihuahua."

"A *chihuahua*?" Belle looked nearly delirious with glee.

"Are you sure?" Alex asked. "Belle can be...a handful."

Fred stood, holding his hand out to the girl. "I'm sure she'll be an absolute angel. Won't you?"

"Yes! I promise! *Please,* Mommy."

"Five minutes," Alex allowed. "That will give Mrs. Winchester and I enough time to finish our coffee. But then you have to come right back, no whining."

She watched them walk away, the burly silver-haired gentleman with her daughter skipping alongside him, and felt her eyes mist. This was what grandparents were *supposed* to be like. When Alex's long-ago classmates had talked about baking Christmas cookies with "mimi" or going fishing over spring break with "papa," she'd envied them their extended families. As she'd grown older, she'd consoled herself with the hope that at least her own children would someday have that cross-generational bond she'd missed. Yet here she was, hiding her daughter from her grandparents.

Dorothea also watched the pair go. "Now that we don't have little ears at the table, may I speak frankly, dear? I hope this isn't too forward, but my son seems quite taken with you. Does my old heart good!"

"Th-thank you," Alex said uncertainly. "Zane is a very special man, and you should be proud of him. But we're not...involved, exactly. We're just neighbors."

"Yes, he was quick to point that out, as well, once he realized just how much he'd been talking about you. His interest in you is far more than neighborly."

"He said as much," Alex admitted. "But Belle and I are in delicate circumstances. She still misses her father, has nightmares about his death. It might not be healthy for her to become overly attached to another man right now."

Dorothea ducked her head. "Oh, I shouldn't have put you on the spot. Fred's always fussing that I'm too nosy. But where my son's concerned… You're a mother. I'm sure you understand the need to look out for your child."

"Completely."

"No matter what happens between the two of you, it's a relief that he's taken romantic notice of someone again. It's been so long since that horrible Valerie, and I was afraid he'd never get over it. Not that he's still hung up on her," she was quick to add. "But he struggled with getting over her betrayal. He was sensitive when he was younger, always bringing home stray animals in need of rescue, standing up for smaller kids who got bullied. It's true that Valerie had a rough home life, but is that any excuse for her becoming a calculating, manipulative liar?"

Because Dorothea paused, Alex obligingly answered "no," but it was clear the question was rhetorical. Zane's mother had made up her mind about his ex-wife years ago.

"He wanted to believe that, with enough love, he could help her, like one of the abandoned puppies he found homes for or the injured baby bird he'd nursed to health. I suppose his teenage hormones and her being gorgeous complicated matters."

Alex squirmed in her chair, uncomfortable with hearing the personal details of his past. "Mrs. Winchester, are you sure you should be telling me all this?"

Dorothea considered the question. "Yes, I believe I should. Because I want you to know what a good thing it is you've done. Zane doesn't have a deceptive bone in his body. My boy is honest to a fault, and he just couldn't wrap his mind around her lying and infidelity. When he finally had no choice but to accept that she was far more duplicitous than he could have guessed... The whole debacle left him so disillusioned I was afraid he would never trust again. But now he's met you."

Her misplaced faith was like a paper-cut across the heart, each word a small but brutal slice. Alex scraped her chair back and rose. "The cookies and coffee were wonderful, but Belle and I really should be going. If you could point me in the direction of your friend's apartment?"

Dorothea nodded. "I hope we meet again soon, though. Perhaps we can all have dinner at my son's."

Doubtful. Even though she'd promised Zane she'd consider his offer of a date, after this eye-opening conversation with his mother, Alex knew she couldn't do it. He wanted her to explore the possibilities of what could happen between them—but she already knew the inevitable conclusion they'd reach.

Zane liked for the good guys to win and for stories to have happy endings. Theirs wouldn't.

WHILE BELLE WAS IN HER dance class on Thursday, Alex distributed birthday party invitations to the other waiting moms. Other than her fellow aspiring ballerinas, the only friends Belle wanted at her party were the Winchesters and a seven-year-old named Trixie Hollinger who lived one street over. Trixie and her mom often passed the house while Trixie practiced her bike-riding skills, and Nicole Hollinger had brought Alex a cheesecake to welcome her to the neighborhood.

Last night Belle had suggested adding two more guests to the list. "Shouldn't we ask Zane's mom and dad? He might be sad if they're not there."

"No, it's a party for kids," Alex had said. "Even though Eden's a big kid, she still counts. Are you sure you're not just trying to get an extra present out of it?" Then she'd tickled her daughter to divert her, pasting on a smile even though she felt depressingly unscrupulous.

Alex had lain awake staring at the ceiling and wondering if it would be better to wait until after the party to turn down Zane—which seemed unfair to him—or to get it over with as soon as possible, even though that might create friction between them at what was supposed to be a festive celebration. There were a lot of things wrong in Belle's young life, and Alex was determined her daughter would have a fun birthday.

At the ballet studio viewing window, Alex tried to cheer herself up by watching her daughter run from one corner of the studio to the other, doing a succession of jumps across the middle of the floor. Other girls stood in line waiting their turn, all of them smiling while Tess called out encouragement. When the cell phone in her pocket rang, Alex stepped away from the window.

"Hello?"

"Hey." Zane's voice was tense. "Do you have a minute?"

"Sure." Had he heard about her meeting his parents yesterday? "I'm just waiting for Belle to finish up dance class."

He wasted no time getting to the point. "There's a kidnapping situation a couple hours south of here, and I've been called in to help. Rangers have jurisdiction across county lines, and the suspect is affiliated with a gang I've studied. I can call Mom and Dad to see if Eden can stay with them overnight, but since the school bus doesn't exactly go to the senior center—"

"Of course she can stay with us! Do you have any idea when you'll be back?"

"Hard to say for sure. I'll leave her a message at the school and let her know you're expecting her. Thank you, Alex."

Belle was ecstatic when both Eden and Dolly came over that afternoon. The little girl played out back with the dog while Eden phoned a classmate about their Shakespeare assignment. Afterward, the teen helped Alex chop vegetables for the salad.

"I don't actually mind reading Shakespeare," Eden said, sounding surprised by this discovery. "Once Beckie explained a few of the jokes to me, I realized some of his stuff's pretty funny. But I can't believe Mr. Gruen is making us stand up in front of the class to perform memorized monologues!"

"I took an entire semester on the Bard in college," Alex reminisced. "I've always loved his plays." She'd never seen one performed live until Chris had taken her to *Romeo and Juliet* for their first date. In hindsight, maybe she should have taken the double suicide as a bad sign.

"I've been thinking about college lately." Eden flushed. "I know, I'm only fifteen, but—"

"It's never too early to plan ahead! I think it's great. Are you trying to decide what type of schools to apply to?"

"More like I'm trying to decide if there are any that will take me," she mumbled. "I've really screwed up."

Alex put a hand on the girl's arm. "Like you said, sweetie, you're fifteen. Most mistakes at your age are fixable. It's not too late, as long as you make a real effort over the next couple of years. Are you willing to do that?"

Eden nodded emphatically. A moment later, she added, "I like Leo and this group of girls in my lit class. They ask my opinion and treat me like I'm smart. They don't just use me as a lookout so they can shoplift jeans. I still miss California, but most of my 'friends' there haven't even bothered to answer my emails. Do you think they just liked me because I thought up the best excuses for teachers and Mom usually had enough alcohol around that she didn't notice if a little bit went missing?"

"If that's what they appreciated about you, then they're idiots."

"Guess my hanging out with them was pretty idiotic, too." Eden lowered her head, her hair swishing forward to obscure her glum expression. "I just felt really alone. Dad was back here…I don't have brothers or sisters. Mom can be cool sometimes, but mostly she's on her own planet. I wanted to fit in, be close to people."

"Been there," Alex said ruefully. She often thought that was why she'd fallen in love with Chris—not because he was rich or good-looking or flirtatious, but because he'd made her feel truly connected to someone else for the first time. While their marriage had ended in disaster, he'd given her some treasured memories and, more importantly, their daughter. "The thing is, even when we screw up, a lot of times something good comes out of it."

"Like moving here? I didn't want to come, but now, I dunno, I kind of like it. I might even apply to colleges in Texas. Think my dad would be happy about that?" she asked shyly.

"He'd be over the moon." Alex felt so proud of the young woman and couldn't wait to hear Zane's reaction to Eden's progress. While the girls set the table, Alex even reached for her phone to call him but stopped herself. If he was working a kidnapping case, someone's life could literally be on the line. Promising news about Eden's changing attitude could wait.

She and the girls ate spaghetti for dinner. By the end of the meal, her daughter was covered in tomato sauce. Alex gratefully accepted when Eden offered to help run Belle's bath and wash her hair.

Deciding the dirty dishes could wait a few minutes, Alex plunked down on the couch with a cup of hot tea

and the TV remote. Normally her viewing choices re-
volved around having a four-year-old in the house. With
the girls upstairs, she took advantage of a few minutes to watch a sitcom for adults. But she never got the
opportunity to relax. During the commercial break, a
grim-faced reporter gave an update on a hostage standoff, promising more details on the night's later broad-
cast. The preliminary facts were that a woman and her
child had been kidnapped by her ex-boyfriend, an al-
leged gang member, and two of his associates. As police officers had started to close in on the kidnappers,
the criminals had holed up in a small family restaurant,
taking the staff as hostages.

Alex sat bolt upright on the edge of the sofa. Was this
the situation Zane had mentioned? When he'd called
her that afternoon to say he needed to work on a case,
she'd imagined him in a police station conference room
somewhere, consulting in front of a whiteboard. But an
armed standoff involving multiple gang members and
innocent bystanders? Now she was picturing SWAT
teams and a shoot-out.

Oh, God. She rubbed her suddenly damp palms over
her jeans, then turned off the television. Eden didn't
need to see her father on breaking news! She would
worry the rest of the night. Was he all right? Was he
in jeopardy?

When Alex caught herself chewing on her pinky nail,
a girlhood habit she'd long outgrown, she determined
that it was time to clean the kitchen, after all. Keeping
busy—that was key. Her movements brisk, she loaded

the dishwasher, then wiped down the counters with antibacterial cleaner. Twice.

"Girls?" she called through the ceiling. "You about done up there?" She needed the distraction of company.

"Almost," Eden responded. There were footfalls over Alex's head, punctuated by occasional giggling.

Belle is loving this. Alex's daughter had been born via emergency C-section after scary labor complications, but even before then, the OB had suggested gently that perhaps Alex's body wasn't meant for pregnancy. She'd agreed to a tubal ligation after her cesarean. Although Alex had come to terms with having only one child, she'd wondered more than once if her daughter would have preferred being part of a larger family. She recalled Belle's wistful tone when she'd said, *Eden could be my sister.*

Alex hoped the happy memories they stored up during their time here would be enough to help get them through whatever came next.

The girls appeared downstairs, Belle fresh scrubbed with her damp red curls plastered to her face and wearing mismatched pajamas. Eden had also changed into cutoff sweatpants and a faded blue T-shirt that was so big it probably belonged to her father.

"My clothes got a little wet somehow," Eden said wryly.

The three of them played the junior version of a popular board game, and Alex rationalized that, since they had a guest, Belle could stay up a little later tonight. It wasn't until Alex caught Eden smothering a yawn that she realized just how late it was and acknowledged that she was using the kids' company to keep from obsessing over Zane. *Bad mother.*

"It's been fun, ladies, but I think it's time for people to turn in. And by people," she said, tapping the end of her daughter's nose, "I mean you."

She supervised as Belle brushed her teeth, then tucked her into bed.

"Can Eden read me a story?" Belle pleaded.

"Just one. And it has to be short."

After Belle was asleep and Eden had retired with a young adult novel, Alex turned on the news, lowering the volume to a barely audible decibel. She wished Zane had called this evening, so she'd know he was all right, but he was busy trying to save lives right now. Her heart went out to the victims, especially the young mother who must be terrified for herself and her child.

The anchorman reported that the kidnappers had fired shots earlier in the day, grazing one federal agent, but all of the hostages were purported to be alive and well. The reporter also cited an interview with an unnamed source who'd said the kidnapped woman was an informant against the gang, that the kidnapping had been retribution. Alex stayed glued to her television, praying for a safe outcome, but between updates, her eyes grew heavy.

At some point, she must have dozed off, because she was asleep when her cell phone rang at 4:00 a.m.

ZANE COULDN'T REMEMBER ever feeling more tired—his fatigue went straight down to his soul. He could have stayed at a hotel for a few hours, got some sleep, but he knew he wouldn't start to feel better until he was back with his daughter. *And Alex.* It had been a foolish impulse to call her at this hour, but he'd wanted to check in and tell her he was almost home. More, he'd needed to hear her voice.

Unsurprisingly, there was no answer. He was about to give up and hit End when he heard her sleep-fogged "Hello?"

"I'm sorry for waking you," he began. "I—"

"Zane!" Her drowsiness had evaporated. Now she sounded alert to the point of manic. "You're okay! You *are* okay?"

"I am. Physically, anyway." Not everyone had been as lucky. Two officers had been injured, and Benita Lopez, the woman who'd been kidnapped yesterday morning, was in critical condition. One of the gang members had been killed.

"It was that kidnapping the news was covering, right? I didn't let Eden see any of the reports, but I watched them on and off until I conked out during a commercial. I was *so worried* about you." Her voice had taken on a wobbly edge.

"I'm sorry for scaring you." His conscience pricked him. "I should have made time to call sooner."

"Zane, you were working to save lives. Reassuring me was not top priority."

Her easy acceptance of his career warmed him. It had been a source of contention in his marriage, that his hours were erratic and some of his jobs were dangerous. "Thank you. And thank you for looking after Eden."

"We loved having her. She was no trouble—in fact, she spared me the usual trouble of making dinner alone and trying to hustle Belle into bed. And Eden said some things tonight about school that are going to make you very proud."

A lump formed in his throat. When they'd been fired on tonight, he'd been forcibly reminded of how much Eden depended on him. Before, with her living so far away and their seeing each other so rarely, he'd been subconsciously convinced that it wouldn't make much difference in her day-to-day life if something happened to him. Having her under the same roof made him feel vulnerable in a way he hadn't previously. But he also felt damn lucky. At the end of a hellish nine-hour standoff, he had people to come home to, people who cared and gave him hope during the dark moments. Until now, there'd only been Dolly.

"Zane? Are you still there? Don't you dare fall asleep at the wheel!"

"No worries, I'm pulling into the subdivision now."

"What? You didn't tell me you were that close."

He heard shuffling and a metallic jangle, then the slight squeak of a door. Up ahead, he saw the spill of light from her porch. His ingrained sense of chivalry suggested he apologize for disturbing her, tell her to go back inside out of the cold and that he'd see her in the morning. But he couldn't. Because what he wanted most in the world right now was to hold her. He swerved into the Comers' driveway and barely had the truck in Park before he swung open his door.

Alex apparently needed to see for herself that he was unharmed because she hurried to him. He caught her in his arms, then bent to kiss her. Beneath the ministrations of Alex's sweet mouth, the ugliness and uncertainty of the day melted away. He groaned, deepening the contact between them, reveling in how good it was even while becoming frustrated that it wasn't enough. She fisted her hands in his shirt, hauling him closer, but his weight almost unbalanced her.

As if they were once more on the dance floor together, he pivoted, turning them so that she was against the truck, giving her a way to brace herself.

"Ow," she muttered. "Side-view mirror." Still kissing him fervently, she fumbled behind them with one hand and managed to open the door.

He briefly considered pointing out the warm house just a few yards away, but then decided he couldn't stop tasting her long enough to make the trip. He'd already journeyed too long tonight to make it back to her. Sparing a brief but grateful thought for whoever invented bench seats in trucks, he climbed inside the cab with Alex. Gone was any reserve she'd shown around him in the past. She straddled him in her desire to get closer, kissing him hungrily. Lust was dulling the edges of his brain, but he was still cognizant enough to register that her behavior had a frenzied undertone to it. She was shaking—with desire, or from her earlier fear?

"Hey." He pulled back slightly, cupping the side of her face and meeting her gaze. "I'm okay. I promise."

"I know. But I also know—" Her voice broke, and he stroked her shoulder as she regrouped. "I know that tragedies occur and people die young. If anything had happened to you…" Unable to finish the thought, she rained kisses over his skin, putting her feelings into actions instead of words. She nibbled a line down the side of his neck, making him even harder. He hesitated, wondering how far she intended this to go.

Alex reached for his hand and placed it on her breast. The feel and shape of her beneath the thin cotton nightshirt, the tight bead of her nipple hardening for him, zapped away the last of his coherent thinking. Everything was sensation and emotion, moments and touches each blurring into the next as he succumbed to his need to explore her. She eagerly raised her arms as he tugged her shirt free, then rocked against him as he suckled her. Her gasps and raw moans spurred him on, and he wasn't sure which one of them reached for the button of his jeans first.

His one moment of sharp clarity came when Alex lowered herself on him. She was wet and ready but so tight it took his breath away. The instinct to thrust home warred with the sudden grave realization that they were unprotected. "Wait." He gripped her hips, loving the lushness of her body. "I don't have…" Her muscles contacted around him, and he gritted his teeth at the exquisite agony. "We're not using—"

"Oh." She blinked. "Condoms? I haven't done this

in so long I didn't even consider…" She sounded flustered and self-conscious.

He rubbed his hand over the small of her back reassuringly, but soothing became caressing as he dipped lower and lower. Her voice was husky and distracted when she added, "I can't get pregnant."

"I haven't done this in a long time, either." And he couldn't remember when he'd wanted anyone this badly. "I'm glad I waited for you." Unable to wait any longer, he began moving inside her.

Unimaginable perfection. He wanted it to last forever. Knowing it couldn't and determined to make sure she got just as much out of it as he did, he slid his hand down between them, finding where she was slick and swollen and responsive. Her cries filled the cab of the truck and sent him reeling into his own climax. He said her name, repeatedly, but it was long afterward before he could string together any other words.

Observations about the outside world gradually intruded, such as noting that the last time he'd seen windows this fogged was when he'd busted a couple of teenagers necking in an empty parking lot. He also couldn't help discerning that, as damn good as his body felt, the front seat of the truck had stopped being comfortable. What the hell was he doing, taking her in the driveway like a horny eighteen-year-old? Alex deserved far better.

"I'm sorry. Not sorry we made love. I wanted that with every cell in my body," he said candidly. "But I should have done it differently."

She didn't bother lifting her head from his chest. "No complaints here."

Was she humoring him? "We're in a *truck*." There went any future claims to chivalry.

This time she cocked her head just enough for him to see her lopsided smile. "Think of it this way—at least you don't drive a motorcycle. Then we would've been in real trouble."

Zane threw his head back and laughed, caught off guard by her sense of humor and by the utter joy coursing through him. *I could love her.* Alex was a special woman. Although he didn't know precisely what the future would bring, there was no way he would meekly give her up just because her house-sitting assignment ended.

He threaded his fingers through her hair and kissed her again, softly. "Today was difficult, and I found myself thinking about you. On the one hand, it seemed like a weakness, feeling like I suddenly have more to lose. But knowing you were here made me stronger, too. I don't know what good deed I did to warrant having you in my life."

His words must not have had the flattering effect he'd hoped, because she looked stricken. Something like recrimination flared in her eyes before she tore her gaze away.

"Alex?"

She shook her head, and he heard that half hiccup, half aborted sob that meant she was struggling not to cry.

"Did I say something wrong? *Do* something wrong?"

"No, you're wonderful. Too wonderful." Before he could try to interpret the logic in those words, she raised her face again. "Ignore me. I'm just…emotional. You're the only man I've ever been with, except for—"

"Chris." He traced idle patterns on her skin. Was the guilt he'd seen because she felt wrong about remembering another man after what they'd just done? "The two of you have a lot of history, had a child together. You don't have to pretend like he didn't exist."

But, as was her habit, she backed away from the topic. Then she put actual physical distance between them, wriggling off his lap and reaching toward the door handle on the passenger side. "I should get back inside before either of the girls wake up."

"Or someone sees us." The first predawn rays of light would begin streaking the sky soon. He ran a hand over his jaw, hardly able to believe what they'd just done. "I made love to a woman in flagrant violation of public decency laws." He tried to joke away the inexplicable tension radiating from her. "You should feel very special, you know. It's not many people who could come between me and the law."

She gave him a contorted imitation of a smile and scrambled out of the truck. *So much for defusing the tension.*

"You're a single mother shopping with a gal pal on a leisurely Saturday while someone else watches your kid," Tess recapped. "Shouldn't you be enjoying the excursion more? Because you look like someone on her way to get a root canal."

The two of them were at a mall outside town where Alex was searching for birthday presents—something that might miraculously make up for the fact that Belle was *not* getting a dog—and Tess was scoping out the first bathing suits of the season to calculate "how much poundage" she needed to lose.

Alex slowed to a stop in front of the entrance to a major department store. "I'm not being any fun to shop with, am I? This sounds cliché, but I have a lot on my mind."

"Belle's birthday? This is the first since her father died, isn't it?"

Actually, it was, and Alex felt like a horrible mother for not realizing that sooner. She couldn't bring herself to nod, which would secure Tess's unearned sympathy. But she didn't know what to say, either.

When she looked into the woman's open, understanding face, the temptation to confess her man troubles welled within her. *I was supposed to tell Zane we can only be platonic friends; instead I jumped him in front of the house where anyone in the subdivision could have seen.* Thank goodness her neighbors didn't tend to be out at that hour. They definitely would have had a new agenda item for the next Home Owner's meeting.

If she confessed to Tess that she and Zane had made love, her friend wouldn't see the problem. Explaining *why* it was such a predicament would require an impossible amount of confession. Even if she trusted Tess enough to risk custody of her daughter, Alex wouldn't inflict the burden of secrecy on someone who had been nothing but generous and welcoming.

It was bad enough that Alex—*Heather, dammit*— had to live with her own lies.

"I *should* be thinking about Belle's birthday," Alex admitted. "But I'm preoccupied."

"With Zane?" Tess asked impishly. "Did you ever talk to him about that kiss? Or kiss him again?"

Alex's cheeks flamed with heat.

"I knew it!" After a brief self-congratulatory smile, Tess shook her head. "I swear, they've been putting something in the water around here lately. My friend Lorelei, you. Grace Torres won't admit it, but I think she fell for someone, too. Why do you look bummed? Zane took your daughter to a ball game today, so I assume you two are getting along all right."

Alex made a strangled noise. "You could say that." Arguing was definitely not their trouble.

"You do know you're turning the color of a stoplight?" Tess peered at her intently. Then her jaw dropped. "You guys didn't stop at just kissing, did you?"

"Shhh." Alex glanced around at other shoppers. "Okay, fine. You caught me. We…"

"Were intimate?" Tess supplied, her grin widening.

"Yes! But the 'after' was more awkward than glow. I haven't made love to anyone since my husband."

Until Zane, the *only* man she'd made love to had been Chris, making the experience the other morning surreal. It was unlike anything she'd ever done before, yet still felt incredibly right. At least, it had up until Zane smiled into her eyes and praised her for being more than he deserved, making Alex feel like a worm.

How could she keep deceiving him? Yesterday, she'd had a lunatic moment where she'd considered pouring out the truth to him. But Zane had an obligation to the law. He'd either turn her in or despise himself for not doing so. She couldn't live with either option.

Tess winced in sympathy. "Awkward is rough. But that's common the first time any two people hook up. Maybe the trick is to hurry along to the second time and make a new, more earth-shattering memory."

"I don't think so. Having sex with him might have… been a mistake." The words almost stuck in her throat. Zane was strong and caring with a sexy smile and a refreshing sense of humor. He was more irresistible than chocolate, and making love with him had felt as natural as breathing. Under any other circumstances…

"I really think you two could be good together," Tess said. "Don't miss an opportunity just because something went wrong. After all, you already have that part behind you now. Why not use it as a teachable moment and move forward? I say in for a penny, in for a pound."

Did Tess have a point? Alex was already in so far over her head she wasn't sure she could get any deeper. Even if it had been a mistake, there was no taking it back. Besides, if she broke things off now, after launching herself at him in his truck, might that prompt him to ask even more questions?

You're rationalizing, trying to find a way to keep see-

ing him so you won't get your heart broken. A pointless strategy. She would relish the temporary, immediate joy of being with him, but it was already much too late to save her heart.

Chapter Eleven

Was there a better place to spend a sunny spring Saturday than a baseball field? *In Alex's arms, maybe*. The undisciplined thought sneaked in before Zane could censor it, causing him to cast a guilty glance at Belle. He shouldn't be lusting after Alex while her daughter was seated next to him on the bleachers.

He chugged some cold water from the bottle in his hands and turned his attention to the action on the field. Eden had never expressed much interest in athletics, but this was informal church softball, not a competitive league. When Beckie had called last night to say her team would be short a player because someone had sprained her wrist, he'd been pleasantly surprised that Eden agreed to fill in. This morning they'd invited Alex and Belle to watch the game.

Alex had seemed so hesitant he'd wondered if she was avoiding him, if she was having misgivings about what had happened between them. But then she'd told him he would be a lifesaver if he took Belle to the ball field since her daughter's birthday was just around the corner and Alex hadn't done any gift-shopping yet. Her explanation of why she didn't want to come along made total sense, so why did he feel like he wasn't getting the whole story?

He wished he could better gauge Alex's reactions to him, but sometimes Zane the law enforcement officer was a hindrance to Zane the man. The sad fact was, there had been far more criminals in his life than lovers and being continuously exposed to the worst in people had skewed his view of the world. Often, when he was with Alex, his intuition cautioned that her responses were…off. As if she were hiding something. But what if he weren't experiencing genuine intuition so much as paranoia? After all, as his mother was prone to pointing out, marriage to Valerie had left its scars. Did Zane want to risk alienating Alex by asking her invasive questions or treating her like a suspect? She was an undeniably expressive woman. Most days, he doubted she could lie credibly about her weight on her driver's license.

At other times, though… He'd embarrassed himself by doing an internet search yesterday on the Hunts. He hadn't been able to find a single mention of a Christopher and Alexandra Hunt in Austin, Texas, no newspaper mentions of a fatal accident or an obituary. There were two Christian Hunts—one an orthodontist, the other a local musician with about sixteen followers on his fan page—but they were both very much alive. Instead of appeasing his growing disquiet, he'd walked away from his computer with more questions.

Mercifully, his daughter stepped up to bat, giving

him something else to concentrate on besides his own insanity.

He clapped his hands together, amused when Belle followed suit. "Come on, Eden Jo!" he called. "You can do it!"

Belle's arms fell to her sides and she gaped at him. "Her name's Jo like mine? Mommy used to always call me 'Josie-Jo' before—"

"Before what?" he prodded.

Her expression was as horrified as if she'd just been told her birthday was canceled. She shook her head mutely.

"It's okay, Belle, you can tell me. We're friends."

"I can't tell." Her bottom lip trembled. "I promised. I'm not s'posed to be Josie anymore."

That was such a jarring comment that he lost all focus on the game. What did she mean? Zane wasn't going to upset her further just to selfishly satisfy his curiosity. For all he knew, "Josie" referred to some game of pretend she used to play. Maybe Alex thought she needed to be more grounded in reality and had asked her to quit. Although that didn't sound like the same mom who'd let her wear fairy wings to a neighbor's cookout.

Belle had scooted away from him on the bleachers and kept her gaze on the ballplayers. "Yay, Eden!" she cheered as his daughter swung and missed.

"That was a strike, kiddo. Strictly speaking, strikes aren't good for the team that's batting."

"Oh." She didn't look at him.

"Have you ever been to a game like this before?" he asked, trying to put her at ease.

"No. Daddy watched the Astros on TV. He *promised* he'd take me to a game." She sniffled, clearly on the verge of tears. "But he never did!"

Oh, hell. The last thing he'd wanted was to remind her of father-daughter outings she'd never get to take. He didn't know what to say. Should he call Alex? "He was probably just waiting until you were bigger," Zane babbled. "And it would have taken you a long time to drive to Houston." A long time by kid standards, anyway—it was at least three hours away from Austin.

Belle gave him a what-are-you-talking-about look, so surprised that she stopping sniffing. "We drove in Houston every day! It wasn't long."

The good news was she no longer seemed sad. What did she mean they "drove in Houston?" Maybe they'd visited. Or maybe the Hunts had lived in Houston as a family and Alex had relocated them to Austin after Chris's death. Or they could have lived on Houston Street, and the four-year-old was confused.

Let it go. It was ridiculous for an intelligent man who'd once married the wrong woman to sabotage his relationship with the right one. Alex was the best thing to happen to him in a long time. He refused to screw that up over some disjointed and groundless hunches.

ALEX HAD ALREADY PARTED ways with Tess when Zane called her.

"Eden's team kicked righteous butt," he told her

cheerfully. "The girls are going for a celebratory pizza. We wondered if Belle could join us or if that would spoil your dinner plans."

"Not that I have any. Pizza sounds great." She'd worked up a major appetite today trying to keep up with Tess in a mall. "Why don't I meet you? We can have dinner together, then I'll take her off your hands."

"Now that's a plan." He lowered his voice. "It means I get to see more of you."

She blushed, thinking he'd pretty much seen all of her already, and was glad she was alone in the car where no one could see her reaction. But she was looking forward to his seeing her again. Maybe Tess was right about the restorative powers of a girls' afternoon, or maybe Alex was simply feeling empowered by the ability to make a deliberate choice rather than simply reacting to circumstances, but she'd decided to date Zane. He knew she was leaving in a few months; she'd made no secret of the fact her future plans were nebulous. That should allow them a goodbye where they each got to keep their dignity.

She didn't want to think about the goodbye part now. She'd rather think about what she had. It was a gorgeous sunny day and she was on her way to see Belle, Zane and Eden. By the time she pulled up to the pizza parlor, she was actually whistling.

Zane waited for her on the sidewalk, looking inexplicably sheepish. Taking advantage of the fact that the girls were already inside, she surprised him with a quick kiss hello.

His entire body relaxed, and a smile spread across his face. "So you're really *not* avoiding me, then?"

"What made you think I was? The way I invited myself along to dinner?"

"Right. Point taken. Knew I was being weirdly paranoid." He cupped her shoulders, pulled her to him and kissed her hard. His kiss was as brief as hers had been, but decidedly more thorough. Would it be too wanton if she announced she'd changed her mind about Eden babysitting and hoped the girl could start tonight?

"I have something to tell you," he began. "And I hope you won't be mad."

"You sound like my daughter," she remarked. "You didn't by any chance color on a wall?"

"Not recently. But you could ask Mom if it was one of my childhood transgressions. She's inside," he said ruefully. "Eden and I had invited my parents to the game, but Dad wasn't feeling well. Mom spent most of the day taking care of him before he shooed her out of the apartment and said at least one of them should enjoy some time with Eden. She called me just a few minutes ago, after I talked to you. I know she accosted you at the senior center, and I don't want you to feel uncomfortable."

"Zane, this is your hometown. Your family's lived here for years. You don't owe me an apology or explanation for her spending time with her granddaughter."

"You're pretty terrific, you know that?" He opened the door for her, and she spotted Dorothea at a booth with Belle. They each held a crayon and were playing what looked like a very serious game of tic-tac-toe on the kid's menu.

Belle waved immediately. "Mommy! Mister Zane's Mom showed me how to draw a cocker spanish. Wanna come see?"

"That would be cocker spaniel," Zane translated. "We had one when I was a kid."

As Alex got closer to the table and saw how closely her daughter was nestled to Zane's mom, she sighed, succumbing to the inevitable. "Dorothea, how would you and your husband like to join us next Sunday for a Beautiful Ballerina Birthday Bash?"

ALEX SPRAWLED BACK ACROSS the mattress, trying to catch her breath. "The truck was impressive, but you *really* work wonders in a bed."

Chuckling, Zane reached over to squeeze her hand. She wished either of them had possessed the foresight to turn on the ceiling fan before they'd started. Temperatures had been rising all week.

"This is really decadent of us," she marveled. "It's bad enough I'm over here instead of working on the party, which was the whole reason Minnie Warner volunteered to pick up Belle en route to ballet in the first place. Plus I've probably dragged you away from something critical!"

"Paperwork," he said. "Don't think of it as dragging me away. Think of it as…providing me with a much-needed break so I can return to my task refreshed."

She rolled onto her elbow and propped her face on

her hand. "Speaking of critical, was Benita released from the hospital?" In the days that followed the hostage crisis, he'd told her more about the brave woman who'd tried to help take down a gang. She had wanted a better future for her son and others like him.

Zane nodded, looking relieved. "She's got some difficulties ahead of her, but I believe in her. Benita's strong. People are often stronger than they give themselves credit for. Sometimes we just don't know what we're capable of accomplishing until we're forced to do it."

"Do you think that's true for the negative as well as positive?" Alex bit her lip. The question had slipped out unintended, and she wished she could take it back.

"I don't follow."

She tried to sound nonchalant. "I mean…maybe there are things a person wouldn't ordinarily dream of doing, things most people would see as bad, but circumstances force them into it."

He frowned. "That sounds too much like the excuses cops hear all the time, ranging from 'you don't understand, man' to the time-honored 'devil made me do it.' I don't think there's ever a right reason for doing the wrong thing."

Alex stared at the ceiling, kicking herself. She should have known this would be his attitude, so why had she brought it up? She couldn't look to Zane to absolve her of her sins—especially since he didn't even know what they were.

"I should go," she said. "Birthday preparations to finalize. Belle is literally counting the hours."

"Mom and Dad are really looking forward to it. Since Eden lived on the West Coast for years, they've missed a lot of girlie milestones." He sat, crossing his arms loosely over his knees. The man had terrific arms. And she could stare at those shoulders all day. "Be warned. Given half a chance, they'll spoil Belle rotten."

She wasn't worried. After all, the Winchesters had raised him and *he'd* turned out great. "As long as they don't get her a dog. Cocker spanish or otherwise." She looked over the edge of the bed, scouting through assorted pillows and clothes for her shirt. They'd been in something of a hurry since Eden, who'd stayed after school to work on a group project, would be home in about half an hour.

"What about Belle's grandparents?" Zane asked unexpectedly.

Her throat went dry. "What?"

"She seems to really respond to my folks, and it got me to wondering. I know you don't have family, but what about Chris? Surely he had a family. Unless he was an orphan, too?"

Could she make that plausible? That she and Chris had met in the foster system somehow and had bonded over their common backgrounds? Had she ever said anything to Zane that would contradict such a story? Her thoughts churned as she tried to recall.

What the hell are you doing, fishing for more *lies to tell him?* Disgust filled her.

"He did have family. We're not close." She yanked her shirt over her head and got to her feet. "You know that night you made me dinner and said my husband's bad behavior and subsequent crash weren't my fault? They took a different opinion. I don't like discussing it."

"Of course you don't." Zane fell back on the bed. "I apologize for prying. I just… Alex, I want to feel like I know you."

She glanced back, trying to keep the rising fear out of her expression. "You *do*. You know the stuff that matters. Maybe we haven't learned all the trivial, but that's what a relationship is about, right?" She clenched her fists to keep her hands from visibly shaking.

"Logically, I agree with you."

Uh-oh. "And illogically?"

"If I didn't know better, I'd swear you were in witness protection," he joked. He was teasing, but there was a grain of something uglier. Resentment? Suspicion? Both possibilities tore at her.

I'm losing him already. "One question," she allowed anxiously.

"What?"

"I really do have to go—your daughter will be home soon—but we have time for one personal question." The concession was for her as much as Zane. She wanted to feel closer to him, too. She hated the invisible walls between them. "Fire away."

"All right." He turned to study her, his gleaming eyes so intense that she pitied any suspect or witness he interrogated. "Can you explain a nickname to me? Your daughter says you used to call her Josie Jo. Where did that come from?"

Hearing her daughter's real name spoken aloud was a blade through her. *No! We're supposed to be safe. No one's supposed to know.* Why had he chosen this moment to ambush her with that? She stood, collecting her shoes without bothering to put them on.

"That's private." Did he notice the hysteria creeping into her tone?

"Dammit, Alex." Frustration roughened his voice to a growl. "Everything's private with you. Everything's too personal to share. Except your body, I guess. You'll sleep with me—you just won't trust me."

She drew back, stung. "You're the second man I've had sex with in my entire life! Don't make it sound like I'm indiscriminately free with my body."

"Freer than you are with your secrets," he shot back. "Some days I catch myself obsessing, what is she keeping from me? Then I think, *everything.* You say this part of a relationship is for getting to know one another, but when I try, you shut me out. You change the subject, you refuse to answer questions, you get hostile. Or, over the last couple of days, you kiss me and the question gets dropped. I think I prefer the direct hostility. It feels more honest."

Tears blurred her vision. A dozen scathing replies came to mind, but she choked them all down. She didn't have the right to argue, because she'd been a fraud from day one. Instead, she mustered as much dignity as she could for a woman trying to shimmy into her pants.

"I'm obviously not ready for this," she said, walking away from him. "Maybe I never will be. Maybe I'm damaged goods. You're a great guy, and you should hold out for someone with more to offer."

"Alex, wait—" He scrambled off the bed.

She paused in the doorway and gave him a sad smile. "On the bright side, you won't have to worry about my distracting you with kisses anymore."

ZANE WOULD HAVE FOLLOWED her, but, given that she was already dressed, she'd had a substantial head start. He couldn't very well chase her naked out onto his front lawn. Besides, say he caught up with Alex…what then? From the first, he'd been the one making a case for them to be together. He couldn't keep pushing.

Look where that had landed them.

It wasn't just his assertive attitude that had driven her from the house, though. He sat on the edge of the mattress, head in his hands, and reviewed the facts. When he'd asked about the nickname, she'd gone green for a second. He'd only seen two other people look like that. One had been a lieutenant on a choppy deep-sea fishing expedition, the other had been a buddy who'd celebrated a hard-earned bust with far too much tequila. As soon as she'd heard "Josie Jo," Alex had looked physically ill.

He could no longer avoid the reality that she was hiding something. The only question was, why? How much trouble was she in? He was beginning to think that he didn't just need answers for himself; he might need them for the sake of her safety and Belle's. He'd already tried searching public records for information on Alexandra and Chris Hunt, of Austin. Maybe he should see if anything turned up for a Christopher and Josie. In Houston—Company A territory. Zane had a good friend who was a Ranger out of Company A.

Maybe it was time to give him a call.

Chapter Twelve

It was the following night, late Saturday, before Zane got the information he wanted—although that wasn't quite accurate. No man *wanted* to learn that the woman he'd been falling in love with was a liar who was currently in contempt of court.

His friend emailed the data but followed up with a phone call. "I didn't ask yesterday why the request and, like I promised you, I won't mention this to anyone. But judging from what I turned up, are we looking at Eileen and Phillip Hargrove again?"

The powerful couple had been on the periphery of an investigation into an allegedly corrupt public official. That investigation had eventually collapsed, with not enough evidence to press charges, and the Hargroves themselves had never been under direct investigation. But there were plenty of people in law enforcement who considered them persons of interest.

"Not at this time," Zane managed. "Thanks for sending me these links. I owe you a beer next time I'm in Houston, okay?" He disconnected while his buddy was still saying goodbye, reeling from the proof of Alex's—Heather's—betrayal.

Although Zane wasn't nearly as talented as the forensic artist who worked with the Rangers, he'd done a few police sketches on the fly. Once he'd scanned his drawings of "Alex and Belle Hunt," it hadn't been difficult at all to find out who they really were. There were numerous pictures of Heather—with longer and much redder hair—alongside her late husband and parents-in-law at social functions; a birth announcement for Josephine Hargrove; an obit for Christopher. Each new document was like an iron spike to his chest.

He was glad Eden had already turned in, joking that she'd need extra energy for Josie's party tomorrow, because Zane needed to be alone. He had a lot to think about and didn't trust himself to be civil company. At the irony, a raw laugh scraped his throat. Not trust *himself*? Too damn bad he hadn't been more distrustful of his beautiful conniving neighbor. That would have saved him a lot of trouble—and possibly have saved his heart.

THE BRIEF FLICKER OF FEAR in her eyes gave Zane a moment of savage satisfaction. He stared her down from the other side of the threshold. Could she tell from his expression that he knew? Before he could say anything to her, Belle appeared to see who was at the door.

Josie, he corrected himself. Josie was already in her fancy pink-and-white ballet dress even though the party wasn't for another few hours. "Mister Zane! Did you come over to give me my present early?"

That gave him a pang, the reminder that today was her big day. He wasn't a monster. He didn't relish ruining the birthdays of five-year-olds. "Actually, honey, I'm here to talk to your mama."

Alex—God, even knowing the truth, it was difficult to think of her as anyone else—squared her shoulders and set her jaw for battle. "Go upstairs, punkin, and make sure your room is clean. You want to have space cleared for any new toys."

The little girl didn't argue, but she did turn very slowly from one adult to the other, as if detecting the strain between them. Once Josie was out of earshot, he followed Heather inside.

"I'm surprised to see you," she said, voice strained. "I thought you understood that Friday afternoon was goodbye."

"Turns out, there are a lot of things I don't understand." His soft drawl didn't mask the menace in his tone. "I was raised in an old-fashioned community where neighbors know each other, look out for one another. At the very least, they introduce themselves. Let's try this again. I am Sergeant Zane Winchester. And you are?"

Her eyes were wild, her hands trembling, but her voice was calmer than he'd anticipated. "I think you know the answer to that."

Yes, but she owed him the truth from her own seductive lips. "I'd like to hear it from you, Mrs. Hargrove."

She blanched, sinking blindly into the chair behind her. "Nothing good will come from my telling you.

You've probably convinced yourself you're here for justice, but you look like a man hell-bent on revenge. I'm not going to fight with you. My baby is upstairs."

Even though she was unquestionably terrified, she showed gumption. He shouldn't be surprised. After all, she'd had the spine to thwart Eileen and Phillip Hargrove. He might have felt a twinge of pride if he weren't so infuriated. He'd made love to this woman, had breathed her name while inside her, and it had all been a lie. The rage he'd felt when Valerie cheated on him, the blinding wrath at being so stupid, flooded back. Would he ever fall for someone who didn't make a fool of him?

Heather claimed he wanted vengeance, but what equitable turnabout was there for what she'd done?

"You should have told me," His voice shook with betrayal. "I could have helped."

"Because men who only see life in shades of 'right' and 'wrong' so often assist failure-to-appear fugitives?"

"Eileen and Phillip Hargrove have been peripheral suspects in two different investigations over the past five years. If we'd worked together, if you'd trusted in the system…" *If you'd trusted me.*

"Like Benita Lopez?" she challenged. "She tried to do the right thing, and it almost got her and her son killed. If you know what kind of people the Hargroves are, then you understand why I can't risk losing Josie to them. What would you do if it were Eden? Wouldn't you do everything in your power to save her?"

He was momentarily stymied by her words. Granted,

Valerie had never been under suspicion of blackmail or bribing public officials, but she had a slew of other vices. Nonetheless, he'd let her traipse off with his only child. Should he have fought harder to keep Eden? *Perhaps—but you would have fought legally.*

Heather Hargrove couldn't say the same.

He looked around the kitchen, belatedly reminded that this house belonged to friends of his. "What do the Comers know about you? I can't see them turning their place over to a complete stranger, but they wouldn't harbor a liar, either."

He saw another flare of panic in her golden eyes, which she tried to cover using sarcasm.

"I'm not answering any questions without my lawyer present," she said tartly.

He pounded a hand on the kitchen island. "Do you get that you actually *need* a lawyer? Do you comprehend the seriousness of what you've done?"

"Of course I do!" she thundered, abandoning her vow not to argue with Josie upstairs. "For days on end, it was all I could think about. And then *you* got added to the mix, and every day has been this toxic stew of regretting my impulsiveness and struggling not to fall in love with the lawman next door."

Some spark of tenderness tried to ignite, but he ruthlessly extinguished it. He wasn't here to kiss and make up. "Heather, you've got to turn yourself in."

Her head jerked up at the sound of her true name, unshed tears wavering on her lashes. Then she slumped, as if all the fight had drained out of her. "Is that a threat?

Like, I've got twenty-four hours to get myself down to the station or you'll drag me there in cuffs?"

"Don't make me out to be the bad guy." His entire life, all he'd wanted was to do the right thing. "I'm thinking of you and Josie. You can't keep running. The longer you try, the worse it will get. Have you thought about how many more lies you'll need to tell? I'm not here to drag you anywhere. If…"

The words were so foreign to his nature that they stopped abruptly, like the lead car in a twelve vehicle pileup. But somehow he continued. "If you try to run, I won't stop you."

"You won't?" Her eyes narrowed, as if she were looking for the catch.

"No." Was he granting her that unheard-of leeway because he knew the Hargroves might actually be dangerous or because he so desperately hoped Heather would do the right thing? "But I'm praying you won't bolt again. Far as I can tell, you and I both married selfish people who disregarded rules and conventions. Is that the legacy you want to carry on for your child, the example you want to set?"

Silence hung between them.

"I could put in a good word for you," he said stiffly. "Like a character reference. Especially if you have any information we can use about the Hargroves."

Conflicting emotions battled across her face. "You've said your piece. Now please go."

"All right." There was nothing more he could do here. As he'd learned the hard way, he could only help people who wanted assistance, those who wanted to change. He was no longer in the business of rescuing damsels in distress against their will. "I'll leave."

The real question was, would she?

THE MINUTE SHE SHUT the door behind him, Heather flew into a flurry of unproductive action. She was trying to be everywhere at once with no clear plan, scurrying to the closet to retrieve the suitcases she'd stored, searching for her cell to call Bryce. *I should warn him.* Through Kelsey Comer, Zane could easily track down the friend who'd aided Heather. Bryce was an accomplice or an accessory—whatever the official term was for a good friend who'd taken bad risks.

Heather had trouble believing Zane wouldn't report her. Although he'd said he wouldn't interfere, she knew what it was like to make a decision under duress and regret it later. How long did she have before his lifelong duty to the law trumped his feelings for a short-term lover who'd lied to him?

We have to get out of here.

"Punkin? I need you to put your shoes on," Heather called up the stairs. "Now!"

Josie appeared on the landing. "Is it time for my party already?"

The eagerness in her expression brought tears to Heather's eyes. *She's already left one home, and I'm uprooting her again.* What kind of mother was she?

A desperate one. Children were resilient. Surely Heather could make this up to Josie over time.

"We have to take a trip. We're going…on an adventure."

Apparently, it was too close to the words she'd used before they came here because Josie's face crumpled. "We're going away? Do I have to be someone else again?"

The question skewered Heather. *Oh, my God.* Her five-year-old was already versed in aliases and false identities. Was this the kind of life she wanted for her daughter? Heather knew the Hargroves were amoral people who would ruin Josie given enough time, but what in the hell was *she* teaching her kid?

"I'm sorry, punkin." Tears washed down her cheeks, and she realized that she wasn't apologizing for leaving. She was apologizing in advance for staying…and for whatever consequences that brought. She knew how furious and disappointed Zane was, but the man she'd fallen in love with was ultimately a good person. No matter how much he might despise her right now, she'd take her chances with him any day over Eileen and Phillip.

ZANE DIDN'T ENTIRELY understand his motivation for driving to the ballet studio. Did it stem from not knowing how to explain the situation to Eden or morbid curiosity for how this would play out? He wanted to believe that Al—that Heather would be there.

You know she won't be. Yet he loaded Eden and their gaily wrapped birthday gift into the truck just the same.

As he drove, memories assailed him. He recalled Heather's hysteria at the festival when she couldn't find her daughter, the affection on her face whenever she mentioned Josie. He'd accused her earlier of continuing the tradition of being thoughtlessly selfish, but even he had to admit that wasn't true. Heather had acted on what she believed to be her child's best interest. She was unquestionably wrong, of course, but her motives weren't beyond comprehension.

Would a judge take that into account, grant her any kind of leniency? There was no actual warrant for her arrest, but if she turned herself in, at the very least, there would be stiff fines. Had she blown her chances of winning any custody case? There was a difference between knowing Eileen and Phillip were dirty and possessing incontrovertible evidence.

Distracted by his jumbled thoughts, it took him a moment to notice the old beater in the studio parking lot. *Her car.* Had she… He tried not to think the question, afraid to let hope rise. But it was too buoyant to tamp down. Had she stayed, then? Was she planning to surrender herself to the authorities and place her faith in the system he fought for every day?

He jumped down out of the truck. "See you inside," he told his daughter abruptly. "I, ah, need to talk to Alex!"

Eden looked amused. "Geez, Dad, I thought *I* was supposed to be the one at the mercy of hormonal highs and lows. I don't even get this worked up about seeing Leo."

Zane raced into the building, spotted Heather immediately. She was hanging balloons with Tess and Nicole

Hollinger while Josie giggled in the corner with Nicole's daughter Trixie.

Heather's eyes widened when she saw him. She made some excuse to her companions and met him in a far corner of the room. "I didn't expect you to be here," she said softly.

"Funny. I was going to say the same thing." But there was more wonder in his tone than accusation. "Are you only here because it's your daughter's birthday?" For all he knew, the bags were packed in the trunk of the car and Heather planned to steal away like a thief in the night.

"I'm here because you were right. This isn't the life I want for her." She swallowed. "Actually, it *is*. We're surrounded by great people, a warm community, neighbors who care. It's everything I always wanted and hoped to one day have. And now I'm going to take all that away from her? If I'm going to dodge the law and teach her that the rules don't apply to her, I might as well just drop her off on Phillip and Eileen's doorstep. At least with them, she'd have the added benefit of her own swimming pool."

"I'm so proud of you. I'm still pissed. And I doubt I could ever really trust you again. But you're doing the right thing, and that's commendable."

"Thank you." She took a deep breath. "I know that what we had... Well. That's over. But is it too late to ask for your help?"

"I'll do what I can," he promised gruffly. He just hoped it was enough.

BRYCE SQUEEZED HEATHER'S hand in the posh reception area, offering one last bit of reassurance before she went in to see her lawyer. When Heather had called to make the appointment, the attorney's secretary had said she was under orders to patch Ms. Hargrove through immediately in the event they heard from her.

"Do you know what you've done?" the lawyer had demanded. "We might have had a shot! You've completely screwed up my case." But after he'd calmed, he admitted that her coming back of her own free will *might* carry a tiny bit of weight with the judge.

Just as she'd apologized then to the lawyer, she apologized now to Bryce. "I am so sorry for all of this. Is Kelsey speaking to you yet?"

"No, but she'll come around. I'm her favorite cousin," Bryce said confidently. "Besides, she's an incurable romantic. She lives for happy endings and hopes you get one. She might have forgiven me already except that her husband the military man is a stickler for rules. To say he's unhappy is an understatement. What about you? Spoken to Zane lately?"

"No."

When she'd first driven back to Houston, Bryce had met her, and she'd sobbed out the whole story. Although she'd omitted the most intimate details, he knew exactly how she felt about the Ranger.

When it came to helping her, Zane had been true to his word. He'd set up an informal security detail, making sure she and Josie were watched. After what she'd done, Heather couldn't completely discount that the Hargroves would try to take Josie without the assistance of the courts. Zane had also used her journal to shift the focus of a cold investigation. If anyone could find the evidence needed to take down her former in-laws, she believed it was him.

But she wasn't out of the woods. Even if the Hargroves were sent to prison for their natural lives—a lovely fantasy—that didn't mean Heather would automatically live happily ever after with her daughter. An extreme judge might rule that Heather serve some jail time, as well. *Some gene pool we provided for my kid.* She could only hope that Josie's time spent around Zane would rub off on her.

There were far worse role models to have. And few better men in the world.

ZANE STARED OUT THE BACK window into his yard, scowling at the rain. *April showers. What a cliché.* He hoped Eden had taken an umbrella with her when she'd left with Leo and his mom. They were having an impromptu celebration at Leo's house because both teens had earned A-pluses on their all-important research papers. Eden had been giddy about her achievement, except for a brief moment when she'd said, "I wish Alex—I mean, Heather—had been able to read it. She loves Shakespeare, you know."

As far as people like Eden and Tess were concerned, Heather Hargrove had been in an unofficial form of witness protection. Zane had fudged some of the details, telling them just enough to let them draw their own conclusions. Only with his mother had he been brutally honest, revealing the entire sordid story. She'd answered with a sad "I see," and had mercifully never broached the subject of Heather or Josie again.

Yet, whether she mentioned them by name or not, Zane felt as if his failed relationship had been present in the subtext of every conversation he'd had with Dorothea ever since.

"Eden mentioned she's going to a sleepover this weekend. How would you like to meet your father and I for dinner in town?" Translation: "We're worried you shouldn't be alone right now."

"We had a lovely game of bridge with the Fowlers last night. You remember their daughter Dinah?" Translation: "Don't give up hope. There's a woman out there who's right for you."

He had no interest in seeing other women, not when he was still so banged up over the last one. This week, he thought he'd made improvement, not thinking about her nearly as much, but then he'd received a call yesterday afternoon from a fellow Ranger based out of the Houston field office.

"We'll be able to press charges against those slippery bastards this time!" the man had gleefully reported. "We questioned a guy Heather had mentioned in numerous entries and he offered to tell us everything he knows in exchange for immunity. That woman has a pretty good memory for details. Between her journal and her agreement to testify when all of this goes to court, she's been a real asset."

When other Rangers had looked at her notes, that's what they'd seen—an asset. Zane read between the lines, though. He knew her journal was a firsthand look into how miserable she'd been for eight years, the things she hadn't wanted to see for the sake of her marriage but ultimately couldn't erase from her memory. She'd run because she was scared of the Hargroves and now that he had a better idea of some of what they'd been involved in, Zane couldn't entirely blame her.

If she hadn't gone on the lam, he never would have met her. Whatever else had happened, he couldn't bring himself to regret having known her.

"Dad?"

Zane started. Had he really been so lost in thought he hadn't heard Eden come in? *So much for your keen senses and well-honed reflexes, Sergeant.* "What are you doing back so early?" He glanced past her. "Where's Leo?"

"We said goodbye on the front porch. I thought bringing in my boyfriend would be…a little insensitive to you. Why flaunt our goopy happiness?"

Great. His fifteen-year-old pitied him. "Did you have fun at his house?"

"Yeah, but…" Eden leaned against the counter, fiddling with the napkin holder and not meeting his eyes. "This is going to sound lame."

"Try me." Zane had learned that the sentiments his daughter deemed lame were often his favorites.

"I didn't want to celebrate with them. I mean, I thought I did, and Leo's parents are pretty cool even if they are superstrict, but I wanted to come home and celebrate with you. *You're* the one who believed in me and put up with me when I was stomping around the house, annoyed that I couldn't get my paragraphs exactly the way I wanted them."

He laughed. "You do stomp. But I love you, anyway."

"Love you, too." She hugged him. "I'm glad I came to live here."

He squeezed her tight, so grateful that he got to see her every day. "I told you this town has a lot to offer when you give it a chance."

Eden nodded. "Do you…do you think Heather and her daughter will ever come back to town? They seemed to like it here, too."

Zane sighed, hating to disappoint her but refusing to offer false hope. "We've talked about this, honey. This was never their home."

"It could have been," she muttered mulishly. "Have you talked to her since she left?"

"Not directly. She's gone back to her real life and has a lot to sort through."

"But you miss her."

Since it didn't really sound like a question, he opted not to respond. But the answer echoed in his mind. *Every damn day.*

Chapter Thirteen

Spring had passed through Texas and, judging from the May heat, summer was officially here. As Zane sweated by the grill, he asked himself why he'd caved to his mother's unsubtle hints that he should invite them over for a cook-out. Currently Dorothea was stepping onto the back deck. She'd probably ask him some question about whether there was anything else that needed to be prepared inside. But they both knew she was really coming to check on him. She constantly sought ways to monitor him, to ask if he was all right without ever voicing the question. Not for the first time, he thought mothers would be uniquely qualified for undercover work.

"Food's just about done, Mom. I—"

"We've just realized we don't have any of that steak sauce your father loves," she informed him, her expression oddly serious for a woman discussing condiments. "Eden and I are going to run to the store."

"Now? But we'll be sitting down to eat in just a few minutes. I marinated the meat. The steaks will taste fine."

Dorothea had already turned back toward the house.

"You don't know your father and this steak sauce. In fact, I'd better take him with us to make sure we get the absolute right kind. Oh, and there's someone here to see you. Bye!" She moved with impressive speed for a woman her age, leaving him flabbergasted.

Based on the facts he'd been given—that his mother was acting like a lunatic and that his entire family had abruptly abandoned him minutes before a family dinner—there were only two logical conclusions to draw. Either his mother had engineered this entire meal as a stealth blind date, which he wouldn't put past her, or... *Alex.* The phony name was simply force of habit. As was the imprudent wash of joy that accompanied it.

Caught between hope and dread, he stepped inside. "Hello?"

"In here." The voice from the living room was painfully familiar, although the woman seated on his couch was slightly less recognizable.

Everything he'd thought or felt in the past couple of months collided in his brain; questions and recriminations and declarations that he'd missed her tangled into an inarticulate mass, leaving him only with the inane, "Your hair sure grows fast." The bright red was beautiful.

"I can't wait until it's long again," she said wistfully. "That short, bobbed cut was never me."

An awkward pause followed. He wasn't sure what to say to the reminder that she hadn't been completely genuine.

"I have Josie," she informed him suddenly. "I mean,

not with me. She's staying at Bryce's, where the two of them will probably play video games nonstop. But the judge ruled in my favor. We won! She's safe."

"That's wonderful." He wanted to pick her up and swing her around in his arms. He settled for smiling.

"It probably helped that Eileen had a total meltdown in court, viciously laying into her lawyer, the judge and her husband. Another factor in my favor is how distracted Phillip and his attorneys are by charges that have come up against him. Saving his own ass is always going to take precedence over fighting for his granddaughter. Thank you, Zane."

"Just doing my job. I'm thrilled for you and Josie, but you didn't have to drive all this way to tell me. You could have called." It was a personal question disguised as an unrelated observation; he'd been learning the art from his mother.

Heather stood. "I'm in town for a number of reasons. I interviewed for a job, and I've been looking at some apartments."

"Here?" The floor seemed to tilt beneath his feet. Getting over Heather was impossible enough when she'd been in Houston. If she was going to be local, he would never be able to move on. *Do you want to?* There was also the question of what she wanted.

"Did I ever tell you I was an art major?"

He shook his head mutely, still trying to absorb the possibility that she might be moving to the Hill Country.

"I was a docent at a museum when I met my late husband. Aside from diligently working on a number of art fundraisers, I haven't been able to use my degree much. But that's going to change. I'll be working at a gallery about twelve miles away. Josie is beside herself with excitement. Tess is, too. She swears Josie has a future as a prima ballerina and Tess wants credit someday for 'discovering' her." As Heather wound down, she began fidgeting, twisting her hands together. "What about you?"

"I don't know anything about ballerinas."

She swallowed. "No. How would you feel about us being around? I know it's not always easy to tell, but I'm a fairly old-fashioned girl. I believe in family and community and getting to know one's neighbors. In that spirit, I thought I should come over and introduce myself." She walked toward him, extending her hand. "Heather Conner. I, uh, went back to my maiden name."

He met her halfway. "Nice to meet you." Touching her in this small, platonic way was torturous bliss. He felt like a starving man who'd just been given a bite of his favorite food—but only one bite. The threat of famine still clung.

"Zane?" Although she withdrew her hand, she stepped even closer. "I know you have reason to hate me—"

"I don't hate you." He'd had a lot of time for his anger to subside. "I understand. You were trying to protect your daughter."

"Does that mean you forgive me?" she asked hoarsely.

How could he not? As they'd discussed multiple times, he believed in fresh starts, the ability for people to learn from their mistakes and change. Not that he wanted her to change too drastically—he'd fallen in love with the woman she was.

He looked her in the eye. "I love you."

"Zane." Her lips parted in an expression of shocked joy.

"I've tried to fight it since you left, but nothing's worked, so I might as well face it. And forgiveness is part of love." As time with his formerly estranged daughter had taught him, relationships could be repaired if people truly wanted to make amends and were willing to work for it.

Heather flew into his arms. "I love you, too. But I would understand if you need more time to think about our relationship. I had planned to ask you on a no-pressure date to find out if our feelings had changed, just one night to see how it could be between us," she said, echoing back his own past words.

"A single night? Not a chance," he murmured against her mouth. "I know exactly how good it will be between us, and refuse to agree to anything so temporary. You're just going to have to stick around this time."

She pushed up on her toes to kiss him back. "There's nowhere else I'd rather be."

"Considering it's been weeks since you guys moved back here," Eden scolded, "I can't *believe* this is your first trip to The Twisted Jalapeño! It's my favorite restaurant."

The refinanced and remodeled Jalapeño had enjoyed a grand reopening in May. Grace Torres was running the place with her new fiancé, another hotshot chef. Ben had told Zane last week, "They're so much alike, it's a wonder they don't kill each other. Not like me and Amy. We're more a case of opposites attracting."

Josie leaned forward in her chair to swipe a tortilla chip through the salsa. "This looks funny. Shouldn't it be red?"

"Not always," her mother said. "This is salsa verde. Broaden your horizons."

When Josie asked what a "horizons" was and Eden tried to explain, Zane grinned inwardly, wondering if his future stepdaughter had found her new word of the week. Since he'd yet to propose, he supposed it was technically premature to think of Josie as his daughter, but he couldn't help it. He was too damn excited about popping the question tonight and spending the rest of his life with Heather.

It wasn't a question of two like-minded people finding each other or two opposites completing one another. For him, it was about understanding and acceptance. They knew each other. They admired one another's qualities and tolerated each other's quirks. He finally had a relationship in which two people were unreservedly honest and connected.

"When do we get to open presents?" Josie asked.

Heather, the guest of honor, laughed. "You weren't this impatient on *your* birthday. We should wait until after the food."

"What?" Zane didn't think he could wait that long to give her the ring box in his pocket.

"Not you, too," Heather scolded. "At the very least, we have to wait for the rest of the party to arrive!"

Tess would be coming, of course, as well as Kelsey and Dave Comer and Kelsey's cousin Bryce. Because Heather spoke so fondly of the man, Zane had worried he might feel a twinge of jealousy when he met Bryce Callahan. Surprisingly, he'd liked the software innovator a lot—although, for the whole day after they'd been introduced, Zane found himself battling the inexplicable urge to pepper conversation with "dude" and "pshaw." The computer genius wasn't what he'd pictured.

"Can we go up front to watch for everyone?" Josie asked. "Eden can come with me."

"If she wants to," Zane allowed. "But you do know that staring at the parking lot isn't going to make them get here any faster?" Just like all the times he'd pulled the diamond ring out to look at it at home wouldn't bring his wedding day any closer. Still, the rush it gave him was downright addictive.

Heather watched the girls thread their way between tables, then stiffened. "Oh, no."

"What's wrong?" He immediately craned his head, scanning the room to locate the source of her distress. For the past month, she'd been the picture of happiness, and he wanted tonight to be perfect.

"The PTA president just stopped Josie to say hi. That woman has scary evil powers. Ever since I went to the school to register Josie for kindergarten next fall, the head of the PTA has been signing me up to chair projects."

"Have you tried telling her no?" he teased.

"Ha! Spoken like a man who's never had to deal with her. If she were in charge of Eden's high school PTA, you'd be singing a different tune." Heather slid down in her chair, ducking her head so her bright coppery hair partially obscured her face. He didn't have the heart to point out that hair like hers was a natural beacon. "Does she see me? Don't look directly at her! Be discreet."

"Bad news," he said. "She's coming this way."

"Damn. Look, if at any point in the conversation, you see me about to nod, will you rescue me?"

His heart swelled with love. Did she know that, in a lot of ways, *she'd* rescued *him?* "Always."

* * * * *

REQUEST YOUR FREE BOOKS!

2 FREE NOVELS PLUS 2 FREE GIFTS!

Harlequin®

American ★ Romance®

LOVE, HOME & HAPPINESS

*What happens when a Texas nanny learns she is
the biological daughter of a prince? Her rancher boss
steps in to help protect her from the paparazzi, but who
can protect her from her attraction to him?*

Read on for an excerpt of
A HOME FOR NOBODY'S PRINCESS
by USA TODAY *bestselling author Leanne Banks.*

Available October 2012

"This is out of control." Benjamin sighed. "Well, damn.
I guess I'm gonna have to be your fiancé."

Coco's jaw dropped. "What?"

"It won't be real," he said quickly, as much for himself
as for her. After the debacle of his relationship with Brooke,
the idea of an engagement nearly gave him hives. "It's just
for the sake of appearances until the insanity dies down.
This way it won't look like you're all alone and ready to have
someone take advantage of you. If someone approaches
you, then they'll have to deal with me, too."

She frowned. "I'm stronger than I seem," she said.

"I know you're strong. After what you went through for
your mom and helping Emma to settle down, I know you're
strong. But it's gotta be damn tiring to feel like you've
always got to be on guard."

Coco sighed and her shoulders slumped. "You're right
about that." She met his gaze with a wince. "Are you sure
you don't mind doing this?"

"It's just for a little while," he said. "You mentioned that
a fiancé would fix things a few minutes ago. I had to run it
through my brain. It seems like the right thing to do."

She gave a slow nod and bit her lip. "Hmm. But it would cut into your dating time."

Benjamin laughed. "That's not a big focus at the moment."

"It would be a huge relief for me," she admitted. "If you're sure you don't mind. And we'll break it off the second you feel inconvenienced."

"No problem," he said. "I'll spread the word. Should be all over the county by lunchtime. No one can know the truth. That's the only way this will work."

Coco took a deep breath and closed her eyes as if preparing to take a jump into deep water. "Okay" she said, and opened her eyes. "Let's do it."

Will Coco be able to carry out the charade?

Find out in Leanne Banks's new novel—
A HOME FOR NOBODY'S PRINCESS.

Available October 2012 from Harlequin® Special Edition®

SPECIAL EDITION

Life, Love and Family

Sometimes love strikes in the most unexpected circumstances...

Soon-to-be single mom Antonia Wright isn't looking for romance, especially from a cowboy. But when rancher and single father Clayton Traub rents a room at Antonia's boardinghouse, Wright's Way, she isn't prepared for the attraction that instantly sizzles between them or the pain she sees in his big brown eyes. Can Clay and Antonia trust their hearts and build the family they've always dreamed of?

Don't miss

THE MAVERICK'S READY-MADE FAMILY

by Brenda Harlen

Available this October from Harlequin® Special Edition®

www.Harlequin.com

HSE65697